Freedom Calls

Journey of a Slave Girl

By
Kem Knapp Sawyer

Kem Knapp Sawyer

WHITE MANE KIDS
SHIPPENSBURG, PENNSYLVANIA

This White Mane Books publication
was printed by
Beidel Printing House, Inc.
63 West Burd Street
Shippensburg, PA 17257-0152 USA

The acid-free paper used in this book meets the guidelines for
permanence and durability of the Committee on Production Guidelines
for Book Longevity of the Council on Library Resources.

For a complete list of available publications
please write
White Mane Books
Division of White Mane Publishing Company, Inc.
P.O. Box 152
Shippensburg, PA 17257-0152 USA

Library of Congress Cataloging-in-Publication Data

Sawyer, Kem Knapp.
    Freedom calls : journey of a slave girl / by Kem Knapp Sawyer.
        p. cm.
    Summary: In 1848, in a bid for freedom, a fifteen-year-old slave girl secretly boards the
    Pearl, docked on the Potomac River at Washington, D.C.
    ISBN 1-57249-206-6 (alk. paper)
    1. Afro-Americans--History--Juvenile fiction. [1. Afro-Americans--History--Fiction. 2.
    Slavery--Fiction. 3. Abolitionists--Fiction. 4. Pearl (Whaling bark)--Fiction.] I. Title.

PZ7.S2683 Fr 2001
[Fic]--dc21

                                                                    00-051251

PRINTED IN THE UNITED STATES OF AMERICA

To Jon, Kate, Eve, and Ida

Contents

Chapter I
The Pearl

April 15, 1848

"Have a little more soup before you go," Louisa's mother said, pouring another ladleful into her bowl. Louisa tried hard to swallow. It would be a long time before she would eat a good meal again.

Neither of Louisa's parents spoke much while they ate. Louisa figured the less they knew the better. If anyone questioned her parents later, they would have nothing to hide. Better they know only that she was leaving, but not any of the particulars. *Do they think I am doing the right thing?* Louisa wondered. *Surely they must. After all they're not trying to stop me.*

"I best be heading out now. Don't want it to get so dark that I can't find my way," Louisa told them. She stood up from the table and looked around the room knowing she might never return. Her baby brother was sleeping soundly on the bed. His arm was flung back and his little head rested against the crook of his arm. Louisa touched his tiny hand. She still marveled at his fingernails.

Her father took great pains to stand despite his bad leg. He crossed over to her and placed his hands on her shoulders. Then he looked her squarely in the eyes. "My little Louisa, we love you so," he said. He planted a kiss on her forehead.

Her mother removed her shawl from her shoulders and wrapped it around her daughter. "Keep this with you. You may need it," she said. She threw her arms around her daughter and pressed her to her warm body. Salty tears slid down her soft cheeks. "I almost forgot," she said, turning to pick up a satchel of food and handing it to Louisa. "Something for nibblin'. I'se expect you'll be hungry before you know it." She dabbed her eyes with her sleeve, "We'll be praying for you."

Louisa moved to the door. Her mother's bonnet hung on a peg beside it. She pulled the shawl tightly around her and, clasping the satchel in one hand, opened the door. The sky had darkened, but in the waning light she could still see. She walked outside and glanced back over her shoulder only once. Her father and mother stood arm in arm.

Louisa made the long trip to the wharf by foot, first along the cobblestone streets of Georgetown, and then across the open fields that hugged the mighty Potomac River. The long tall grass reached her knees. After walking so far and so fast that she grew breathless, she found the landmark she was looking for, a small house, painted white, which gave the spot its name, White-House Wharf.

Docked behind the house was the *Pearl,* the boat that would take her north to freedom.

The *Pearl* was not expected to leave until close to midnight. Louisa clasped her knees to her chest and waited hunched on the grassy hill overlooking the wharf. From her perch she watched two young men board the boat. They carried several parcels and moved quickly as they lowered themselves into the hold of the ship. A man—she had a hard time making out his face—held the hatch open and quickly closed it behind them. Others arrived soon after, some by foot and some by wagon.

Louisa recognized the driver of the wagon—his name was Judson Diggs. He'd given her rides before when she was running late. Judson had many friends and he liked to talk. *People would have been better off walking here,* she thought. *Best not to let anyone in on our plans.* She certainly hoped he'd be able to keep their secret.

Louisa looked back over the fields she had just crossed. Her shoes and ankles were caked with mud. She didn't want to start the journey this way but she had no choice. It could be days before she would have a chance to wash her stockings. In the distance she could barely see the roofs of the buildings in Georgetown. *I ain't goin' to see these houses no more,* she thought. She was leaving behind both her parents and the slave quarters in the senator's house where she was born and raised.

Her parents worked for the senator and Louisa had always assumed she would do the same. But on her twelfth

birthday the senator sent her out to work for Mrs. Frye.
That was three years ago. Mrs. Frye paid for her services,
yet every dime Louisa earned went straight to her master.
Today, she had finished a full day's work, pressing and
folding piles of clothes and linens. She had washed the
floor on her hands and knees until the pine boards
gleamed. Now, she didn't have to be bothered with all that.
She had shut the door to her mistress's house expecting
never to return. Whatever work the future held for her, it
wasn't going to be laundry. No more burning her hands
with scalding water or wringing out clothes dripping with
bleach that stung her skin. All that lay behind her now.

Still there would be people she would miss—her
parents and baby brother, and her friend Abby, a white
girl who lived on the same street as Mrs. Frye. *I mustn't
think about them now,* she thought. She got up and started
walking down the hill, telling herself not to look back.
Dusk had turned to night and the houses in Georgetown
had faded into darkness.

Louisa climbed up on board the deck of the *Pearl* and
was greeted by a small man with a reddened face and a
bandanna tied around his grizzled hair. "Chester English
is my name. Welcome aboard, young un'." The man kept
talking as much to himself as to her. He grumbled that
whatever happened he did not want to get caught. He
wished the captain had stuck to delivering wood and hadn't
"gone and got mixed up with slaves." Working in the dark

and keeping secrets did not appeal to him. It certainly was not what he bargained for when he agreed to come to Washington. He was just a cook. He did not mind doing a few extra things like loading the wood on and off the boat. All he wanted was to earn enough money to feed his wife and child. Why had he let himself get dragged into this scheme? Where was the captain anyway? If he did not come back, Chester was going to be in real trouble. Louisa listened to him mutter, watched his sour face, and pondered, *Do I really know what I'm getting into?*

An older couple followed Louisa onto the boat. *If it weren't for Pa's bad leg, he and Ma might be here too,* she thought. Some of the passengers were moving down into the hold, but Louisa wanted to stay on deck for the departure. As still more people boarded the boat, she was pushed against the edge. Only the railing kept her from falling overboard.

When the deck was so full that Louisa thought the boat could not possibly hold another person, Captain Daniel Drayton and his co-captain Edward Sayres arrived. They barked out a few orders to Chester English. He quickly and deftly untied the boat's fastenings. As the *Pearl* slid smoothly over the water, the passengers on deck raised their arms in the air as if to cheer. But the fear of being caught was so great that the cheer was a silent one. Louisa looked at the two captains. One, stern-faced, studied his equipment. Louisa thought she caught a glimpse of a smile on the other. This must truly be a bold man. And yet he looked like an unassuming sort. He sported a scruffy beard, his shoulders drooped, and his back was rounded. If he stood up straight, he wouldn't be an inch taller than five feet six.

Louisa gazed out at the water sparkling with the reflections of the stars above. Gentle waves rolled up against the side of the *Pearl*. For years she had dreamt of freedom, but that desire, though heartfelt, was undefined. There was no plan, no who, no when, no where. And then, just last Thursday, she overheard a conversation and, as she listened, she thought, *My dream, it really might come true.*

It happened on her way home. She had just left Mrs. Frye's and, when she neared Pennsylvania Avenue, she heard the band's drum roll. Hundreds of glimmering lights shone in the darkness. As she drew closer, she saw that the mysterious light came from the flickering fire of torches. She recognized many of the people who had poured out onto the streets, senators and ordinary citizens, tavern keepers and doctors, coopers and cabinet makers, lawyers and clerks, merchants and ministers, their wives and families. At first the cause of this celebration puzzled her. Then she remembered the talk she'd overheard at home. The senator was explaining to his guests that the French had deposed their king and they spoke of giving all men the right to vote. Several congressmen planned to give speeches to commemorate the birth of the French Republic.

Louisa walked towards the Capitol where the band was playing. She stopped to join the crowd gathered to hear the speeches. Senator Foote from Mississippi promised "the universal establishment of civil and religious liberty" and "the emancipation of man from the fetters of civil oppression." The words she heard were quite beautiful and stirring, but at the same time they made her sad. She knew those words rang hollow for anyone with African blood. White people rejoiced for their French brothers, but ignored the African men and women who worked by their side. It was as if they saw right through them.

"You may never get another chance like this one," Louisa heard the man next to her whisper to his neighbor. She listened more closely and learned that he was trying to convince his friend to run away with him. He had heard that a boatman from New Jersey was willing to take fugitives north. They planned to depart on Saturday evening. The friend had only a short time to make up his mind, but it would not take long to prepare—he would be allowed to bring with him little more than the clothes on his back. Louisa couldn't believe her ears. Here was a slave planning to escape by boat and he was suggesting there was room on the boat for more!

Suddenly, Louisa found herself asking if she could come too. She did not think about missing her parents or putting herself in danger or losing her friends or getting caught. She just blurted out the words before she had time to consider the risks.

"I couldn't help hearing what you was saying and I'se wonderin' if you think I could come along," Louisa said. She had never done something so daring in her life. She never talked to strangers and she had never given very serious thought to running away. It had always been a vague possibility, but not something that appeared likely— a fantasy, that was all. Now here she was talking to this man about escaping.

And then she'd actually gone and done it. Here she was two days later aboard the *Pearl*.

"Everyone down below now!" the captain boomed. "No sense pressing our luck." They were nearing Seventh Street and a few lights flickered from the shore. The captain did not want to run the risk of being spotted.

Louisa, squeezed between other bodies, waited in line to descend the ladder into the hold. Holding the skirt of her dress with one hand, she grabbed the top rung of the ladder with the other and carefully eased herself down. Her foot gently grazed the head of a person below. "I'm awfully sorry," she mumbled. She looked around the crowded space, dimly lit by a lantern, and saw the people who would be her companions on the voyage. No one would turn back now. This time they had done more than talk. Every one of them had dared to make the break.

The temperature inside was hot and stuffy, like one of Washington's mid-summer afternoons when the air was so stagnant you felt there was nothing left to breathe. The space was cramped. Louisa could hardly move. All the bodies filling the cabin—and it seemed to Louisa that there must be close to a hundred—pressed against each other. She tried to make herself as small as possible and rested her head on her knees. If only she could get some fresh air or stretch her legs.

"Did you come by yourself?" Louisa heard a voice whisper in her ear. She looked up and peered into the face of the girl next to her. From the light of the lantern Louisa could see a friendly smile.

"I did. What about you?" Louisa answered.

"My sister Mary she come with me," she said, nodding in the direction of the girl on her right. Louisa could make out the figure of another girl crouched nearby. The two sisters appeared to be about Louisa's age. In the dark Louisa could not see any others her own age. But, at the other end of the cabin, she could hear the wails of an infant and the cries of a small child. "My name's Emily," the young girl next to her said. "What's yours?"

"I'm Louisa," she answered.

"You'se mighty brave to go by yourself," Emily said.

Louisa didn't think she was so brave. It was true she was setting off on her own, abandoning Washington, the city that had been her home since birth. It meant leaving behind family and friends, but it also meant giving up work as a slave, endless days of working around the house, doing whatever she was told, and handling other people's clothes. What she said to Emily in the darkness of the ship was, "I don't wanna to spend all my days bending over a scrub board."

"But there ain't nobody to look after you," Emily said.

"I'se been lookin' after myself for a good while now. Mama, she just had another baby," she answered. Louisa remembered thinking how strange it was that her mother did not try to talk her out of going. Instead, she had told her, "You'se young. Your whole life's laying ahead of you." That's what her mother always liked to say. And it was those words that spurred her on.

Louisa felt her stomach rise up inside her as the boat rocked back and forth. Tiny beads of sweat had formed along her hairline. She loosened a button wishing she did not have to dress so warmly. But she had to wear everything she owned because she knew the less she had to carry the better.

If only she could peel off one layer of clothing, she would be more comfortable. The two pairs of thick stockings and the two dresses—the brown everyday dress worn over the pale blue one she saved for Sundays—were about to make her suffocate. The black, fuzzy shawl that her mother had given her did not help matters, but she would never want to part with it. The shawl might come in handy as a disguise, but, more importantly, it would prevent her from getting lonely. When she held the shawl close, she could feel her mother's presence and hear her whispering, "Do what you have to do."

Louisa looked at Emily. Maybe she could make a friend right here on the boat. She was going to need a friend.

Chapter II
The Capture

During the night the wind died and the *Pearl* came to a standstill. Yet no one spoke aloud of fear. The thought that was foremost in every mind, "What if there never is any wind?" was not uttered. Some managed to doze. Others closed their eyes hoping sleep would bring them some relief.

By dawn the breeze picked up. One of the stowaways climbed out on deck and returned with the news that they had just passed Alexandria. The captain followed him into the cabin to distribute bread and water. Then, taking a hatchet, he swung at the bulkhead and knocked an opening into the wall so a few of the passengers could crawl into the adjoining cabin to cook. Louisa never made it into the next room. Too many people in such a tight space blocked her way, but someone did pass her a cup of giblet soup. The warm liquid and smell of cloves comforted her stomach.

As the *Pearl* reached the mouth of the Potomac, the fickle wind grew quite strong. Word spread that Captain

Sayres favored dropping anchor and waiting for the wind to change, something Captain Drayton wanted to avoid at all costs. By now word of the slaves' escape would be out in Washington. "We've got to go where the wind takes us," he urged Captain Sayres. "It's best we head out to sea. We've got to get as far from Washington as we can." He pleaded with him to press on. But Captain Sayres did not want to risk taking the *Pearl* out. They were approaching a narrow tip of land called Point Lookout. Captain Sayres knew of a secluded cove called Cornfield Harbor where they could hide. He was not about to be persuaded otherwise. And though they were both co-captains, the boat belonged to Captain Sayres. He would have the last word.

Daniel Drayton slipped down into the cabin to explain the delay to his passengers. "If the wind changes, we'll be out of here before dawn," he said. "Just hold tight and trust in the Lord."

Louisa knew she should be feeling less queasy now that they were settled in the harbor, but her stomach seemed to be getting worse, not better. Still huddled in the corner of the cabin, she said to Emily, "I'se got to have some fresh air." She tried to steady herself as she stood up.

"I'se going out then, too," Emily said. "You look like you'se about to faint. A bit of cool air 'll do you good."

The cooler night air did help settle Louisa's stomach. In the distance the girls could see the tall pine trees lining the shore. Their branches waved in the air and appeared to dance to the wind's music. "I ain't never seen a sight like this. Why, I ain't seen nothin' so beautiful," Louisa said.

"I ain't never even been out of the city," Emily answered.

"Me neither," Louisa said. "I knew a fella once was makin' plans to escape. He told me he didn't know positively what was out there, but he done know for sure it was beautiful. I remembers him saying, 'There's land out there like you've never seen and there's more of it than you or me can ever imagine. There's land out there that white men don't own. There's land out there that they ain't even touched—that they ain't even walked on.' Now I can see why he said that."

Louisa and Emily leaned on the railing and watched the gulls fly overhead, diving towards the water in swift, graceful motions, and shooting up again, fluttering their wings above the girls' heads. The last time Louisa had seen gulls, she and her friend Abby had fed them bits of bread. That would have been on a Sunday, Louisa's day off, when she and Abby would often walk down to the Potomac and go wading.

A loud male voice interrupted the gulls' squawking. "You girls better climb back down. I don't want anyone coming around the bend and catching sight of you. It's time we all turn in."

Louisa and Emily slid down into the hold and returned to their spot on the floor near Emily's sister Mary.

The day was coming to a close, their first spent in freedom. And, although the passengers were confined to the boat, they felt they had their first taste of liberty. Louisa had been too excited to fall asleep the night before, but on this night, the second of the journey, sleep came quickly.

Yet Louisa would not sleep for long. Shortly before two in the morning, loud screams from on deck awoke all the passengers. Louisa opened her eyes, but could see nothing in the dark. From the noisy commotion above, she knew a group of strange men must have boarded the boat—not a friendly voice among them.

Richard, a young man sitting near Louisa and Emily, weaved his way through the passengers over to the ladder, saying, "We'd best see what's going on." Several other men followed him up to the deck. Within seconds the shouting and the scuffling grew louder. Louisa remained next to Emily and did not move. She was trapped. They were all trapped.

The hatch door opened once again and Richard climbed back down. All heads turned towards him. "They've come for us," he announced solemnly.

"How many be there?" one of the older men asked.

"The number's right high. Why there's more on deck than there is down here," Richard answered. "They've got a steamer tied up next to us and there's even more of them waiting on board. They have us covered."

"But are they armed?" someone wanted to know.

"We don't stand a chance. They have muskets. We ain't got none. They have knives. We ain't got none," Richard replied.

Suddenly Richard felt someone poke something hard into the small of his back. "Put your hands in the air. Slow and steady now. Don't try anything fancy," the man ordered. He was a squat, snub-nosed man with beady eyes and red hair blown helter-skelter by the wind. He spoke as one comfortable giving commands. Richard lifted his arms above his head and the weight of his arms grew unbearable.

One of the intruder's companions swung a lantern into Richard's face, blinding his eyes. Another one called out, "All men up on deck. Women and children—you're to stay where you are. Not a move out of any one of you."

Richard's arms were thrust behind his back and tied together. The captor pulled the jute so tight that it cut into his skin. He shoved Richard towards the ladder, kicking him in the shins and taunting him, "Get on out of here. You're going back where you belong."

Richard did not cry out which only made the man kick him a second time harder than the first. The men left Richard on deck, his arms fastened behind his back, his legs tied to the other captives. They took Captain Drayton and Captain Sayres, bound them, and led them to their boat anchored next to the *Pearl*. They threw the two captains against the railing. Bright red blood gushed out of Drayton's jaw, staining his clothes and the whitewashed floor of the boat.

The captors tied the *Pearl* to their steamer, the *Salem*, and set sail, towing their booty behind. By nightfall they arrived at a fort outside the capital. Eager to make a grand entrance into Washington in daylight, they dropped anchor and waited for dawn. One of the angriest of the men came up to Drayton, leered at him, then spat in his face, and grinned. Rubbing his mouth with the back of his hand, he announced that he thought it best to lynch this man then and there and make no bones about it.

"Wait," one of his companions cautioned. "First, we need to get out of him the names of those who planned this conspiracy. Just who do you think put the idea of freedom in their heads? I see the work of one of them Northern abolitionists."

His friend clearly enjoyed taunting Drayton. He yanked out a knife from under his belt and brandished it under the tip of the captain's chin. "If we take you in alive, you better be prepared to talk."

So great was the anger aboard the *Salem* and so high was the tension that the captives feared they would be killed by the mob waiting to greet them in Washington. As night wore on, the armed men stood vigil. Drayton never drifted off to sleep; he was kept awake partly by the piercing sensation of the rope cutting into his skin, but more by fear of what the morning would bring. Louisa felt sick to her stomach. She would be thrown in jail or taken to the slave pen to be sold. The senator and Mrs. Frye would never take her back. She wouldn't be allowed to see her mother or father or baby brother. She would no longer be permitted to go where she pleased on her day off. In Washington no one cared what she did once her work was done. She had learned to read and write in her spare time. But if she were sent away her fate could be worse. She might be confined to the master's home or made to work all day in the fields. Louisa had fled a terrible situation, and yet what lay ahead was much bleaker. Louisa had gambled and lost.

At dawn the two ships pulled anchor and set sail. The captors had become giddy with the thought of the warm reception they would receive. They expected to be welcomed as heroes. As they drew close to the city, the guards aboard the *Pearl* made all the women and children come on deck so they could be seen from shore. Throngs of people were waiting on land for their arrival. Louisa cast her eyes down, but could not escape the clamor of their victorious cheers. Although no man had ever seen her naked, she felt as if all her clothes were suddenly ripped off and she was exposed to a crowd of ogling ruffians. Louisa wished she could sink to the floor, but she knew that would never be allowed. Her guard poked a stick into her side. "Stand up straighter or I'll break every last rib in your body," he declared.

The *Salem* pulled in at the wharf at Four-and-a-Half
Street with the *Pearl* at her side. Louisa watched the two
captains, now tied the one to the other, descend. The
guards shoved the other captives into lines, yelling at them
to prepare to disembark.

Francis Dodge, the young slave holder who had
organized the chase, kept a careful eye on the men as they
filed off the steamer. Then he signaled to his cohorts on
the *Pearl* to order the women and children to follow suit.
The older children had no trouble keeping up, but the little
ones needed to be carried. A woman with a small child
and baby lagged behind and the guards shouted in anger.
When the baby began to cry the woman snuggled him
against her shoulder, still firmly clasping her child's hand
firmly. "Hush your sniveling," the guard called out.

Large crowds of spectators watched as the boats
unloaded. The guards made the slaves march through the
streets towards the city jail. Word of the fugitives' return
spread quickly. People came out of their homes and shops
to watch as they passed by. Mothers lifted their children
up so they could see. Men arrived on horseback to witness
the event. As the captured fugitives turned the corner, a
slave dealer named Gannon suddenly lunged toward
Daniel Drayton with a knife. The police pulled him back,
but not before he had cut a bloody sliver from the captain's
ear.

Louisa and Emily, walking side by side, shuddered
as they heard the commotion ahead of them in line. The

hordes watching them had multiplied. In her whole life
Louisa had never laid eyes on so many people in one place,
not even at an inauguration. *There must be thousands here,*
she thought. All of Washington had come out to see them.
Several spectators shouted, "Lynch them!" Louisa grabbed
Emily by the arm.

Chapter III
Abigail

While Louisa was sailing on the *Pearl* down the Potomac River to Point Lookout, Abigail Bailey sat on her doorstep. Fourteen years old, she was tall for her age, with long brown hair and sparkling eyes. She lived in a three-story, ivy-covered, red brick house on E Street. Charlie, her dog, a sweet black, brown and white beagle, lay asleep, curled up at her feet. He tucked his head under one paw and every once in a while opened just one eye to check on Abigail. Then he would close it and drift back into a deep sleep, exhaling loudly through his nose.

Abigail—or Abby as she liked to be called—was waiting for Louisa to appear. It was Sunday afternoon and the two girls often spent this time by the river. The first time Abby met Louisa was on a Sunday three years ago. Abby was outdoors walking and felt hot and sticky. She got to the riverbank and stood staring out at the water thinking how refreshing it looked. If she could just feel the water between her toes, she would feel so much cooler. She took off her shoes, peeled off her stockings, and started scrambling down the rocks. At the river's edge, several tall bushes blocked her view, but the intermittent sounds of water splashing made her aware of the presence of another person. She crossed through the underbrush and found a young girl, just about her height, skipping stones across the water. The girl turned, caught sight of Abby and, holding up her skirt with one hand, started dashing up the riverbank.

"Wait, don't go. The river's wide enough for the both of us," Abby called after her. She bent down, picked up several pebbles, and threw them into the river. The girl watched Abby for a few minutes without moving and then returned to the bank. She picked up a rock and tossed it as far as it would go. The two girls took turns skipping rocks across the water, each time trying to out-distance the other.

"I used to come here with my pa to fish, but now my pa's leg gone bad and he can't make it down the bank, so I comes by myself on a Sunday. That's my day off, you see," Louisa explained.

The two girls returned to the river the following Sunday, and before long the riverbank became a regular meeting place. They went wading, climbed on the rocks, and discovered secret passages through the underbrush. Whenever Abby slipped into the river and got her clothes wet, she had to sneak into her house, run upstairs, and quickly change clothes before her parents saw her.

Once a boatman offered to row Abigail and Louisa to one of the small islands on the Potomac River. The island was completely uninhabited, so the two girls could pretend they were explorers. They gathered nuts and searched for wild animals. The boatman returned for them at the end of the day. He offered them some bread and suddenly they realized they were starved. They took the bread and greedily devoured it.

But this Sunday, while Abby waited for Louisa to appear, was different. There was no trip to the island, no picnic, no wading in the Potomac. Abigail looked down the cobblestone road. Louisa was nowhere in sight. *I hope she's not taken ill,* Abigail thought. *Not now that winter is over. It's not like Louisa to stay inside even if she's not well. There's got to be another reason.* Abigail had a sinking feeling that something was wrong.

Abigail overheard Mrs. Swan, the Baileys' across-the-street neighbor, talking to Cora Sands. Mrs. Swan looked well dressed as always. (She was the kind of person who never stepped outside her house without first putting on her hat.) She was saying, "Mary Hale did not show up for work today. I don't know how she expects me to manage what with ten expected for Sunday dinner. And to think that she made no effort to send someone else or to even get a message to me."

Abby wondered if perhaps Mary had run away. *She might never return. Mrs. Swan would never be able to feed ten people for dinner without help.* Then suddenly Abby thought, *Maybe Louisa ran away too! Would she run away without telling me? If she has escaped will I see her again? How will I ever find her?*

Abigail was tall and slender like her mother. She had inherited her mother's smile and her father's brown eyes and dark hair. Her father, Gamaliel Bailey, was born outside Philadelphia, the son of a Methodist minister. He studied medicine, spent some time at sea, and then moved to Cincinnati, Ohio, where he met his bride-to-be Margaret Shands, a native of Virginia and a preacher's daughter. Margaret had always studied hard and liked to read books. She was fond of discussing them with the young men who attended her father's church.

Gamaliel and Margaret were married in a simple ceremony. Since they could not afford a place of their own, Margaret's brother offered them a room in his house. Eventually the Baileys moved into their own home. Gamaliel devoted several hours a day to his medical practice, but he found his heart pulled in another direction. At that time the men and women opposed to slavery were increasing in number. Their movement was gaining in strength and influence. Gamaliel had always stood in firm opposition to slavery. He believed, with every part of his being, that it was wrong and must be stopped. To him the strongest weapon had always been his pen. He wanted to fight slavery with words.

The idea of working for an abolitionist newspaper was born. Dr. Bailey knew he could find men of like mind at the *Philanthropist*. He started work there and within a year succeeded James Birney as editor and publisher. Still, he continued to practice medicine on the side, partly as a means to fund his newspaper endeavor, but also out of a sense of obligation to his patients. He served them well and yet, if his patients noticed that he appeared distracted, they recognized where his true love lay. Although fond of both people and words, Gamaliel preferred words. The newspaper business claimed more and more of his time. He worked long hours and slept little.

Margaret and Gamaliel's first-born child did not survive the winter. The season was bitter cold and the baby's croup never improved no matter what remedies his father prescribed or how many swaddling clothes his mother wrapped him in. But, by the following Christmas, Margaret was ready to give birth again. Abigail did not arrive until the first week in the new year. Marcellus came next, his birth marked by a significant event. The night he was born, an anti-abolitionist mob forced entry into Gamaliel's newspaper office, grabbed his printing press, and tossed it into the Ohio River.

Gamaliel was not about to let this malicious act destroy his newspaper. He bought a new press and resumed publishing. In 1841, anti-abolitionists plunged his press into the river a second time. Gamaliel had the paper going again in only a matter of days.

Five years later, a group of British interested in helping fund an abolitionist newspaper in Washington asked Gamaliel to become its editor. Gamaliel and Margaret were reluctant to move their family, but they both felt that an anti-slavery newspaper could have a greater impact if read by senators and congressmen. A move to the nation's capital would give the abolitionist cause a stronger voice.

The Baileys came to Washington, settling into a house only a few blocks from Gamaliel's office. By now the Baileys had six children—Abigail and Marcellus, Frederick, Bella, Frances, and Frank (still a baby). Dinners were always quite noisy affairs. Both Margaret and the cook saw to it that no one left the table hungry. The cook stayed to tidy up the kitchen after dinner and, on her way home, often had to stop to catch her breath.

The first issue of the *National Era,* consisting of four large pages, appeared on the streets Thursday, January 7, 1847. An annual subscription cost two dollars a year. Interest in the newspaper spread quickly. A wealthy English Quaker offered to pay five hundred dollars a year to support the literary contributions of his friend and fellow abolitionist, the poet John Greenleaf Whittier. Gamaliel was eager to hire this writer with a fine reputation and a devotion to the cause. He also employed Sara Jane Clarke, a twenty-five-year-old New Yorker, who used the pen name Grace Greenwood. Miss Clarke wrote for the paper in the mornings and, in the afternoons, took charge of the children's lessons. If the Baileys had guests she would stay into the evening, helping the children organize Shakespeare skits for the guests' entertainment.

"Abigail!" It was her mother calling her. "Don't you hear me?" Abigail stood up to go inside. She might as well face the fact that Louisa had been detained. For one reason or another her friend would not be joining her this afternoon. Of course she didn't really know that Louisa had escaped. Abby had a tendency to make assumptions. But it wasn't going to surprise her if Mrs. Frye, Louisa's mistress, could not find her. Abby thought, *If Louisa did run away, she can't be very far. There's the old cemetery vault in Georgetown where fugitives sometimes hide, or so Louisa says. Maybe, just maybe, Louisa's gone there. If she's running away, that could be her first stop.*

Later that evening, one of the *National Era* reporters came to the Baileys' house to tell them that a large group of slaves—some said as many as one hundred—had tried to escape by boat. A posse headed by the Dodge boy had gone off in pursuit.

Many city folk assumed that Abby's father was responsible for inciting the fugitives to escape. Rumor spread that he was the instigator. The next day, when friends of the Baileys heard threats that an anti-abolitionist mob might start a riot outside the Baileys' home, they pleaded with the Baileys to go into hiding.

Colonel Seaton, the mayor of the city, and the Baileys' next door neighbor, also suspected that there might be trouble and wanted to look out for Gamaliel and his family. The mayor and his wife urged them to spend the night at their house.

Gamaliel had not wanted to accept Colonel Seaton's offer, but his wife Margaret told him they needed to protect the children. Reluctantly, Gamaliel agreed. Mrs. Seaton gave Abby the room that had belonged to her oldest daughter, now married and living in Boston.

"This room has been empty for too long. It's good to have it occupied again. Let me know if you need anything," Mrs. Seaton had said that evening as she closed the door behind her.

There was no way Abby could fall asleep. Mrs. Seaton had placed a candle on the bedside table and Abby watched the shadows it cast on the wall. Of course she didn't know for sure, but she couldn't help thinking Louisa must have been on the *Pearl*. And she wouldn't be able to rest until she knew Louisa was going to be safe.

Well into the night, as Abigail lay in bed with her eyes wide open, she heard sounds of angry men on the street below. Sitting up in bed, she held back her long brown hair with one hand and cupped the other around the candle. With one quick blow she extinguished the flame. A dribble of wax, tear-shaped, trickled down the side. Abby crept across the room and pressed her body against the wall near the window. She reached for the curtain. Slowly and deliberately, she slid back the cream-colored poplin.

A large group of men, more than fifty, each one appearing on the verge of attack, had gathered on the street below by her family's house next door. Her father stood outside with his arms crossed against his chest, his eyebrows arched, and his forehead furrowed. He wore the same indignant expression she had seen many times when she asked to stay up past her bedtime.

Mr. Radcliff, the spokesman for the group, addressed her father, "We have come with the request that you cease publication of your paper and that you remove your printing press by ten o'clock tomorrow morning. We beseech you, as you value the peace of this District, to accede to our request."

Her father spoke calmly without raising his voice, "You are demanding of me the surrender of a great constitutional right—a right which I have used, but not abused,—in the preservation of which you are as deeply interested as I am."

What has Father done? Why is everyone out to get him? Abigail wondered.

Abigail could hear loud shouting in the distance. *There must be a crowd of people not far from our house.* She thought she could make out the words, "Down with the *Era*," but she was not sure. *They must be coming closer.*

She wanted to cry out to them to go home—"Leave my father alone. He didn't do anything."

In the dark, another voice, this one clear and resounding, threatened to tar and feather her father if he refused to surrender his press. Abby heard her father answer, "Is there a man among you who, standing as I now stand, the representative of a free press, would accede to this demand and abandon his rights as an American citizen?"

"We know we are asking a great sacrifice, but we ask it to bring peace to our city," came the reply.

Her father put his arms to his sides, lifted his chin, and, looking straight ahead, said without flinching, "Let me say to you that I am a peace-man. I have taken no measures to defend my office, my house, or myself. I appeal to the good sense and intelligence of the community, and stand upon my rights as an American citizen, looking to the law alone for protection."

"Abigail! Move away from the window!" Abby's mother had just walked in the room. Abby did not move.

"Mother, I have to hear what Father's going to say. Please don't make me go to bed," she pleaded. Her mother came closer to the window and stood next to her.

"You demand the sacrifice of a great right," her father was saying. "I am one man against many. But I cannot sacrifice any right that I possess."

Abigail was filled with a strange mixture of fear and pride as she listened to her father's words. Her mother had grown silent and was not insisting she go back to bed. Abigail could see the tears gathering in her eyes. She turned away from her mother to look out the window once again. This time she saw the front door opening as her grandfather stepped outside to stand by her father. He was trembling so much that Abby wondered if he was going to hit someone with his cane.

"Go away now," her grandfather ordered. "Don't disturb my son. He has not wronged you in any way. It is time for all wise men to go to bed. Go. Leave this house. You are not wanted here."

Abigail, who wanted nothing more than to stand next to her father, turned to run downstairs, but her mother caught her by the sleeve of her nightgown. "You can't go out there," she whispered.

"Yes I can. If Grandpa can, then why can't I?" Abigail took her robe from the oak bedpost and started to slip her arm through the sleeve.

"You might get hurt, Abigail," her mother warned. "Those men are angry. You never know what might happen."

"I don't like them saying things like that to Father," Abby answered.

Abigail saw her father grab her grandfather's arm. "We must make them understand," he said and, turning to the crowd, added, "Gentlemen, you appreciate my position. I cannot surrender my rights. Were I to die for it, I cannot surrender my rights."

Her father had said all he had to say. With those words he nodded good-night to the crowd and led her grandfather inside, shutting the door behind them.

"Down with the *Era!*" one man shouted. Another yelled, "Now for it! Gut the office!" The men set off in the direction of Gamaliel's office, marching towards Seventh Street.

"What's going to happen?" Abby asked.

"Morning will tell. You must try to go to sleep now. There's nothing to be done at this hour," her mother answered. Abigail slid into bed and pulled the coverlet under her chin. Her mother, holding up her blue skirt in one hand to keep from tripping, bent down to kiss her forehead.

Abigail wondered why her mother was always telling her to go to sleep. Real adventure happened in the dark. Some of her best ideas came to her in the middle of the night. Why did they have to go next door and miss all the excitement? *I don't want to spend the night cooped upstairs. I need to know if Louisa was on the boat. I need to know where she is. And is it true what they said, that the fugitives have been put in jail? Why do these men think Father is responsible for the slaves trying to escape? Mother said he hadn't heard a word about the plot beforehand. Their disappearance was as much a mystery to him as to anyone. Why then are these men so angry? And where has Louisa gone?* The questions tumbled through her head. Abby lay

awake in the strange room for what seemed the longest
time. A driving rain began to fall a little before dawn—at
long last its sound put her to sleep.

Chapter IV
Coach Wheels

"There must have been five hundred people gathered outside the Patent Office, nastiest mob I've ever seen!" Abigail overheard one of the *National Era* reporters talking to her father. He had come running to the house early in the morning to alert her father to the news. "You heard them shout, 'Down with the *Era*! Down with the Abolitionist!' They were after you. They want nothing more than to destroy the press and burn our building and force you out of town. They don't want the *National Era* sold on our streets and they're not going to be happy until they see us gone," the reporter continued in hushed tones, but loud enough for Abigail to make out what he was saying.

During the night, after Abigail's father had turned away the anti-abolitionists sent to taunt him, the men had rejoined the angry crowd outside the Patent Office. Together, several hundred of them marched around the corner to Seventh Street where big, gold letters, spelling NATIONAL ERA, hung across the front of the newspaper building. They banged on the door, heaving their weight against it in an attempt to break it down. They threw stones and bricks and shattered windowpanes.

The noise had aroused the police. Captain Goddard of the Municipal Guard and Philip Barton Key, the United States district attorney, arrived on horseback and ordered the crowd to break up. "Off with you now! You're up to no good!" the captain shouted.

"We want to destroy the press!" came the answer.

Mr. Key climbed onto the horses' water trough and spoke to the crowd, "Gentlemen, fellow-citizens, you know that I am no abolitionist," he replied. "But I call upon you, as friends of law and order, to drop your stones and bricks. The law will remedy any existing evil. The Constitution of your country will bring you justice. Rest assured of that."

"It hasn't done it," one of the men called out.

"On with you now!" shouted Captain Goddard. The rioters knew the captain was not to be trifled with. The men turned to go, leaving behind a few broken windows and splintered furniture, but an intact press.

That night Abby's family returned to their own house to sleep. Abigail once again lay wide awake in bed. Then a sudden noise alarmed her. Had a rock hit the window? Was someone trying to attack the house? Last night's mob wanted to go after Father's press. Did they also want to harm his family? Anti-abolitionists were known to set fire to buildings. Would they come after her house with lighted torches? She looked through the window but saw no broken glass, no flames, no light. The rock was not large enough to do any damage. What could it mean?

Abigail slowly pulled the covers back and cautiously slipped out of bed. She did not want to wake Charlie, the beagle, asleep at the foot of her bed.

Through the window she saw the blackened street and the silhouettes of houses. The leaves of the trees did not rustle. No owl disturbed the quiet. Abby thought she saw a dark, human form standing behind the maple tree. Ghostlike, the figure appeared to raise a hand in the air. Abigail's heart beat faster, breaking the stillness of the night. She could not make out the features in the dark, but that made no difference. She knew who was there.

Abigail flew down the stairs, darted into the kitchen, and flung open the door. Barefoot, she ran towards the figure she had glimpsed partially hidden behind the tree.

"It's you, Louisa. I know it's you," she cried as she threw her arms around her friend.

Louisa, laughing with joy at seeing Abby again, asked, "How'd you knows it was goin' to be me?"

"I just knew," Abby answered. When I first heard what happened, I thought to myself you must be on that boat. I haven't been able to sleep since."

"You'se not the only one," Louisa said.

"I thought they put everyone in jail after they captured the boat," Abby whispered.

"They done that," Louisa answered. "But then they decides to take us over to Alexandria to put us in the slave pen. They start leading us back to the waterfront. They put handcuffs on the men. They don't watch the women and children the way they do the men. That's when I up and run away."

"Weren't you scared?" Abigail asked.

"I says to myself, things ain't gonna be much worse than they are now, so I might as well try. If I can run away once, I can run away twice," Louisa explained. "You'se not goin' believe what I have to tell you."

"You better come inside first," Abby said, as she pulled Louisa towards the house. "Someone might hear us out here."

"What'll your parents say?" Louisa asked.

"We won't tell them," Abby said, grabbing Louisa's hand.

When they reached the kitchen, Abigail whispered, "We'll have to be very quiet. Here, come sit down. I'll just light this candle. If we hear anyone coming, we'll blow it out."

Louisa took a seat on a three-legged stool. Abigail stood on her toes to reach a round tin. She pulled it down and opened it, revealing neat stacks of cinnamon buns dotted with brown sugar.

"Coach wheels!" Louisa exclaimed, her mouth watering. "Just what I wants," she added, as she put one of the buns in her mouth. She thought of the many times she had stood in this kitchen helping Abigail and her mother roll the dough into narrow strips, brushing it with melted butter, sprinkling on cinnamon and brown sugar, and then rolling it back up. She and Abby would take turns flouring the knife and cutting the dough into slices almost an inch thick.

Abigail poured two tall glasses of milk from a metal container. "Start with this," she said.

While Louisa ate and drank, Abigail uncovered the leftover ham, carefully trimmed with cloves in diamond-shaped patterns. She took out the carving knife and managed to cut several thick slices. "I'll get you some chop pickle and some corn pudding. And then we can have pound cake," she said.

"I'se never been so hungry in my life," Louisa answered.

Just then a floor board above the kitchen creaked. Louisa stopped chewing. She felt a lump in her throat and could not swallow. Abigail gasped and let the carving knife slip out of her hand. It made a loud noise as it hit the floor. Louisa and Abby froze motionless. The creaking continued.

"Who's there? Out with you!" Abigail's father shouted from the hallway.

"We can't let Father know you're here," Abigail whispered. Louisa immediately jumped off the stool and crept under the table.

"I told you last night I refuse to surrender my press. Leave a good man alone and be gone," Abigail's father said in a booming voice.

Abby could see the ray of light from her father's oil lamp and her heart beat faster. If she joined Louisa under the table, her father would see the food and look for the culprit. If she faced her father, she might have to lie. She did not want to lie, but she also knew she had to protect Louisa.

"Father," she called, "there's no intruder here. I was just hungry," she said, praying he would not step into the kitchen.

"Abigail, it's you," her father said. Abigail looked up to see her father standing in the doorway. He towered over her—a tall man with a face that did not hide the experience of his years. His brow was furrowed, his eyes deep-set, and his beard graying. She felt her face turn crimson. "Darling," he continued, "what keeps you up at this hour?"

Louisa huddled under the table with her shawl over her head. She mouthed the words, "Please, don't look down" over and over.

"I couldn't sleep, so I thought I'd get something to eat. I always sleep better after I have a little something to eat," Abby answered. She hoped her father would believe her.

"Don't stay up too late and try not to let the stairs creak. You don't want to wake your mother. She didn't sleep much last night," Gamaliel said as he turned to go.

Abigail waited a minute and then poked her head under the table. She whispered to Louisa, "He left. It will be all right now. You can come out." Louisa poked her head up from underneath the table. "Louisa, I can hardly believe you've done what you did," Abby said. "I mean you've escaped twice. Why, once on the boat. And now, you've run away from jail. I just don't see how you could do it."

"Was nothin' really," Louisa answered. "They didn't even handcuff us. They made us leave the jail and they said they were goin' to send us down to New Orleans to be sold. The men, they tied them up and made them walk two by two. But the women and the children, they didn't bother to tie us. One of the guards followed right behind waving a big stick. He kept swingin' it in the air like above his head. I said to Emily—she's this girl I met on the *Pearl*—'I ain't never seen someone act quite so crazy, you know, like he was out to get someone.' I kept wanting to get down real low or cover my head with my hands, but I knew if I done that, I'd just draw attention to myself. And that would be the worst thing to do. Well, this guard saw a friend of his standing on the side of the road. He was watching us go by and calling us all these names—I mean names you've never heard. The guard stopped to talk and suddenly I saw that I might actually have a chance to get away. It ain't like I planned it or nothin'. I just sort of dropped out of line. I guess if anyone were to notice I'd just pretend I was sick or something. I found a hiding place behind an open door. After a while I saw no one was goin' to come after me. But I needed to wait until dark to come over here. I don't know what I'se goin' to do now. They'se sure to do a count and they'll be sendin' guards out to look for me."

Abigail listened to her friend's story. She'd always thought Louisa was daring, but she hadn't known she was this brave.

Chapter V
In Hiding

For two days the citizens of Washington remained on edge. During the day people went about their business, but come nightfall people took to their homes for fear a riot would erupt. Captain Goddard distributed a handbill urging citizens to maintain peace and preserve the honor of the city. Abigail saw the handbills posted on buildings near her house and the newspaper office. These signs made her nervous. They meant her father and his press were at risk. His stomach was bothering him again. Her mother called it dyspepsia and said the last thing he needed was something more to worry him.

Louisa did not dare venture out into the city knowing that talk of the *Pearl* and the fugitive slaves had not died down. Abby wanted Louisa to hide in her room until they could come up with a plan for her escape. She was lucky that her bedroom was the only one on the third floor. Just a year ago she had begged her parents to let her move to the garret. She insisted that since she was the oldest she should have her own room. Her parents and her brothers and sisters slept on the second floor. As long as Louisa did not make too much noise, no one would know she was there. They would not tell Abby's parents for fear they would disapprove. It was not like Abby to keep something this important from her parents, but she had to do it to protect Louisa.

After the first night that Louisa spent hidden in Abby's room, Abby awoke and went down to breakfast. She returned with bread and fruit for Louisa. When Abby left for school, Louisa fell back asleep even though the sun shone brightly through the window. For the past few days she had hardly slept. Now, she was going to catch up.

That afternoon, back from school, Abby ran upstairs, newspaper in hand. "Wake up, Louisa," Abigail whispered loudly as she shook her friend's shoulder. "Look, I brought the paper. You won't believe what's on the front page." She spread the newspaper out on the floor.

The front page of the *National Era* showed a story on the capture of the *Pearl* and the attack on the newspaper office. Her father called the attack on the press an outrage. "We stand upon our rights as a man, and as an American citizen, and will use these rights, in speaking and writing freely upon any subject we please, despite all threats or violence," he wrote. "It is a damning disgrace, that at the very moment we are rejoicing with the people of France at their triumph over a despot who undertook to enslave the press, an attempt should be make to strike down the freedom of the press in the capital city of this republic, in sight of the national legislature."

Another story told how most masters refused to take their slaves back after they were captured. Angered by the slaves' betrayal and shocked by their bravery, they sold them to slave dealers without a care for their future. The slave dealers, Bruin and Hill, took them out of jail on Thursday night and brought them to their slave pen in Alexandria. They threw the men in one room and the women in another. At the end of the week Bruin and Hill planned to send them by ship to New Orleans and put them up for auction.

"I don't know whether the owners are trying to teach the slaves a lesson or whether they're just angry, but it seems like they want nothing more than to get all of you out of town. And they're not giving a second thought to what will happen to you," Abby said.

"I bet they're plain scared that if seventy-six of us could do what we did, we might try it again. We might get even more to come with us," Louisa answered.

Abby thought, *Surely Louisa's decision to run away is the right one. If Bruin and Hill get their hands on Louisa, they'll send her to New Orleans. Her future will be doomed. She could easily end up far away from Washington with a terrible master.* Abby and Louisa would have to come up with a scheme to allow Louisa to escape north. But in the meantime Abby could not let her parents know Louisa was hiding in her room.

Abby's father hated slavery as much as anybody she knew. He did not hesitate to voice his opposition and took stands that were both courageous and unpopular. Everyone at the newspaper knew him to be unflinching and doggedly loyal to his cause. But Gamaliel Bailey also had strong feelings about the best way to end slavery. He refused to do anything he would have to hide. He sympathized with others who took in fugitives, and he could count many such men and women among his friends. Yet he himself refused to take part in any secret activities. As publisher of the paper, he believed he should stand behind his deeds and words so that he could earn the trust of friend and enemy. He wanted to conquer slavery, but he was selective in his choice of weapons. Argument and reason were the ones he would use. Abby had only to look in today's paper for a record of his views: "Whatever we do, we do openly. We cherish an instinctive abhorrence of any movement which would involve us in the necessity of concealment, strategy, or trickery of any kind."

Abigail could understand her father's position, but that didn't mean she agreed with him. Louisa was her friend, and she would do anything to help her—even if it meant going against her father's wishes. But it wasn't an easy choice. She had grown to fear her father's anger, which, although rarely expressed, was formidable. She had hardly ever let him down and had earned his trust over the years. If he discovered Louisa hidden in her room, he would be both shocked and furious.

Her mother, on the other hand, might take a different position. She had witnessed the terrible treatment of dozens of slaves and knew that for many the only hope of a less dismal future lay in a successful escape to a free state. A few of Margaret Bailey's friends not only helped plot escape routes, but also had established hiding places in their houses. Abby thought, *Mother might think I was doing the right thing if only I didn't have to keep it secret from Father.*

It felt strange to do something behind her mother and father's back, and yet Abby knew she had to follow her own conscience. She was doing what she thought was right—helping Louisa to gain her freedom—even if she had to act in secrecy, against her parents' wishes.

For the next few days Louisa remained hidden in the garret. Although Abby's bedroom was the only one on the third floor, it still wasn't easy keeping her brothers and sisters out. Whenever Abby heard someone on the steps, she'd shout, "I'm resting," or "I'll be down in a minute." If they asked her to play, she'd say her head ached. If they insisted on coming in her room, the plan was for Louisa to slide under the bed or hide in the wardrobe, but so far Louisa had not had to do either.

Abby also had to contend with Sara Jane Clarke, the governess. Abby went to school in the morning and took lessons in history and French from Miss Clarke in the afternoons. Miss Clarke met with Abby in the library and assigned long texts to read, grammar to memorize, essays to write, and then gave Marcellus, Frederick, and Bella their lessons. (Frances and Frank were still too young.) Before leaving in the early evening, Miss Clarke would knock on Abby's door to ask if she had any questions. Louisa would quickly step into the wardrobe while Abby took her time coming to the door.

"I understood perfectly," Abby would reply. Sometimes she varied her answer. "It seems pretty clear," she'd say. Of course the next day when Miss Clarke would look over her work, she could see that Abby didn't exactly understand everything but had made several errors. Miss Clarke carefully circled them and patiently explained her corrections, no doubt wondering why Abby had not asked for help.

Only Charlie, the beagle, was allowed to enter Abby's room. He provided Louisa with company and made the long days bearable. *Of course anything is better than going to New Orleans,* Louisa thought. Louisa's mother had been born in New Orleans, and what Louisa had heard made her want to stay away from it.

One night, after everyone in the house had gone to sleep, Louisa told Abby her mother's story. She spoke softly in the dark so as not to wake anyone.

"In New Orleans you can be free one day, but you can wake up the next mornin' and find you ain't free. And if you ain't free, you don't wanna be in New Orleans," Louisa's mother used to say.

Chapter VI
Genevieve's Story

Louisa thought her mother would have been an artist if she had not been a slave. There was something about the way she remembered New Orleans. If anyone called Washington's weather sticky, Genevieve, Louisa's mother, would say, "You ain't seen nothin' until you've been to New Orleans." She'd talk about the beautiful live oaks, and how it would get so hot but then you'd go and sit under the trees and soon your brow would stop sweating, and if there was a breeze then you'd feel pretty close to heaven.

For as long as Genevieve could remember, she had adored flowers. Maybe that's why she became a beekeeper. She'd kept honeybees for years before Louisa was born. Genevieve loved to spend time outdoors and she could also make money by selling the honeycomb in the market on Saturdays. That meant they could usually count on eating well on Sundays. Genevieve always saved half of what she made, but lately she'd used most of her savings to pay the doctor to take care of Louisa's father. Louisa thought raising bees must make her mother think of the flowers of her youth—red rosebuds, orange blossoms, white magnolia blooms, vines of purple wisteria. Genevieve said in New Orleans you saw flowers everywhere you turned. They thrived in carefully plotted gardens and grew wild and uncultivated in the fields and along the riverbank. Every trellis and iron gate was awash with color.

Lizzie, Genevieve's mother, was born a slave. Her master, Marc Brodin, took a liking to her and, on her eighteenth birthday, he freed her. A year later, Genevieve was born, the love child of the two. That was back in New Orleans.

When Genevieve was still little, her mother used to give her money and send her to the market on errands. Genevieve remembered clutching the money so tightly that her fist ached. All the vendors knew her and saved the best produce for their youngest customer. Genevieve could always count on receiving a juicy plum to eat on her way home. Sometimes she made a short detour and wandered into the cathedral. On hot summer days she liked to take off her shoes and walk barefoot on the cool marble floors.

Genevieve was only nine years old when her father went off to fight against the British in the Battle of New Orleans. The day he left for battle, Genevieve's mother took her by the hand and led her outside to say good-bye to her father. He sat proudly on Carmen, his chestnut brown stallion, and lifted her into the saddle. He put the reins in her hands and told her to say "giddyap." After that he gave her a hug and kissed her on the cheek with wet lips, and then held her by the shoulders as she slid off Carmen's side. He bent down to kiss his wife (or the woman he called his wife—Genevieve often wondered if there had ever been a ceremony seeing as how her father was white and her mother was black and that kind of wedding wasn't considered proper). He tipped his hat and rode off. As Genevieve watched him disappear, the last sound she heard was Carmen neighing.

Marc never came home. In a battle that lasted only one-half hour, the Americans gained a significant victory. Two hundred eighty-nine British were killed, and thirty-one Americans. Marc was one of them. Genevieve's mother said he died a hero. Years later, Genevieve learned that when the battle was fought on January 8, 1815, there had been no war. Or rather the war had officially ended. The Americans and British had signed the peace agreement in Belgium on Christmas Eve, but word had not yet reached New Orleans. She had thought he had died for his country, but that was a lie.

Not long after Marc was killed, Lizzie received a visitor, a quite tall, quite dapper man sporting a mustache and brandishing a polished mahogany cane. He informed her that her husband had left behind a sizable debt. Marc owed him one thousand dollars. If she was not able to come up with the money, he would be obliged to resort to extreme measures. He hoped this would not occur, but he would not hesitate to follow whatever course became necessary. "And now I must take my leave. But rest assured, I keep my word and shall return," he said as he departed. Lizzie refused to take his hand.

Lizzie feared that the freedom she thought belonged to her and her child would be taken away from her. She was sure this intruder would find some way to take her and Genevieve as payment for the debt Marc owed him. (Although they had always lived well, she was just now beginning to realize that they lived on credit. Marc was a man of many promises; indeed he might have kept half of them, if only he had lived.) Very much undone, Lizzie called her daughter to her side and told her they should prepare to leave immediately. She explained that they would set out after dark and must travel lightly. "We'll go first to the swamp where no white man will ever find us," she said. They had each other and that was what mattered most.

But Genevieve did not want to leave without seeing her friends in the market one last time. While her mother was upstairs packing, she slipped outdoors and ran as fast as she could to Decatur Street. The market was terribly crowded. The Indians sat on brightly dyed blankets and displayed their woven baskets. Others sold meats and fowl, fruit and flowers from the back of carts. When Genevieve shouted to the vegetable man, she had a hard time making herself heard. He glanced up, but did not see her in the crowd. She turned to cross behind the cart so she could get closer to him. Suddenly an arm grabbed her around the waist. Her body was pressed against the stomach of a burly man with foul breath and a husky voice who panted into her ear, "Screaming will get you in trouble. I don't recommend it."

Genevieve could not have screamed even if she had dared—the man's coat sleeve was jammed into her mouth. He then lifted her onto an orange cart, still holding her roughly and keeping her body close to him, not once removing his arm from her mouth. Only then looking at his face, did she recognize him. It was her father's creditor, the man who had threatened her mother early that morning. The driver, his eyes hidden underneath a wide-brimmed hat, raced off and did not stop until they had left the French quarter far behind. The men dragged her off the cart and tied her to a tree behind a building. The large man beat her. Her tender skin turned red as he snapped the whip against her bare back. Sharp pain, more intense than any she had ever felt, pierced through her. Her skin cracked open and bright red blood flowed from her back. Her head became woozy; for a moment she could only see black and then she lost consciousness.

When she awoke she was stretched out on a cot. She felt weak and could barely lift her head. She heard male voices coming from the other room. She could distinguish the voices of her captors, but did not recognize the third.

Listening more closely, she learned her captors had just completed a transaction—they had sold her to a complete stranger. The first thought that came into her head was that she hoped this stranger would take her away— anything rather than be left in the hands of her captors. A minute later as she still lay on the cot, she realized the significance of the conversation. Suddenly, she was no longer free. The liberty she had known all her life ended with her father's death. The color of her skin would curse her the rest of her life.

Genevieve would have no recourse to free herself. A nine-year-old girl—who would believe her story? The man who bought her from her captors was a slave trader who would take her to Washington. She remembered little of the ocean voyage. The feeling of always being seasick. The cold, wet compresses an old woman placed on her wounded back. The stale air in the cramped quarters on the boat.

In Washington she was purchased by a senator and his wife. At first she had to peel potatoes and polish silver and brass, stoke the fires, and work the garden. Outside labor was what she preferred. Sometimes the mistress would oversee her, but often she left her alone. Genevieve had her own spade and watering can and spent hours weeding and digging. The outdoors sparked an interest in insects. She studied both bees and butterflies.

Genevieve heard nothing from her mother, nor did she have any contact with anyone from New Orleans. She did not lose hope of seeing her mother again and whiled away many an hour imagining their reunion. When she heard a knock at her master's door, she often pictured her mother on the other side. Somehow, she was sure her mother would find her.

As the years passed Genevieve took on more duties in the kitchen and the nursery caring for the senator's growing family. Still, she hoped for a message, the knock on the door, or even the chance encounter with her long-lost mother.

And then one day Genevieve received an omen. A gentleman from New Orleans, a Mr. Beauregard, came on business to call on her master. He had a warm, kind face. When she served bread pudding at dinner, he told her he had never tasted bread pudding quite like hers. When he was about to leave, she brought him his hat and coat and, as her master was otherwise occupied, she took a moment to address him. She said her mother lived in New Orleans, but she had not heard from her in quite some time and she hoped perhaps when he returned he might inquire about her whereabouts. She gave no details about her own capture and did not reveal to him that she had been born free. If she did, he would only assume she was lying and make no effort to help her.

"I would be glad to be of assistance. Tell me her name and I shall make inquiries," he offered graciously.

"People called her Lizzie. She was Marc Brodin's widow," Genevieve answered.

It was only a few months later that the senator's wife died in childbirth leaving behind five children. Genevieve was asked to spend more time in the nursery. Her master took to brooding in the drawing room. He kept a bottle of brandy and a glass by his side.

One evening, after Genevieve had tucked the children to bed and was preparing to help serve her master his dinner, he called her into the drawing room. "Genevieve, I have something for you," he said as he handed her a package. Genevieve untied the string and carefully tore away the paper. Out fell a beautiful beaded purse, blue, the color of the midnight sky. Inside the purse was a letter. Genevieve pulled it out under the watchful eyes of her master. She could not read and he knew this but, respecting her privacy, would wait for her to hand it to him.

"My dear niece," he read. "Not a day has passed without my wondering what became of you. My prayers were answered when I learned of your whereabouts and your good health. Mr. Beauregard, the gentleman you spoke to, returned to New Orleans and attempted to locate your mother. He was directed to me, the closest of kin.

"When you disappeared, your mother was worried sick. For days she combed the city, searching for any trace, any clue. But then she had to take to her bed with a fever. Her temperature rose steadily. She called for me then and my mistress let me go to her. At times her legs shook and she could not control the motion. She knew she would not see you again. She asked that I find you and give you this purse. Your mother received this gift from your father shortly before he left for the Battle of New Orleans.

"Your mother's illness was not drawn out. If it is any comfort, she suffered only for a few days. It was yellow fever that took her life here on earth, but it was to the Lord that she went for everlasting life."

Genevieve's master continued to read for a minute, but Genevieve could no longer make out his words. Her master then bowed his head and, without looking at Genevieve, handed her the letter. He paused and after a moment rose, saying, "Take the rest of the evening off, Genevieve. I certainly don't expect you to—" He didn't finish his sentence, but walked out of the room, leaving Genevieve alone in the drawing room. She sank into a deep armchair. Seven years had passed since she had last seen her mother. For all those years she had harbored one dream and now in only a matter of minutes her dream was destroyed.

"Mama gets a little teary-eyed when she gets to this part about her mother dying and all," Louisa told Abby. "She holds my hands in hers and says that a voice spoke to her and said there was an angel watching out for her. That voice was as clear as mine is now. Mama believed the Lord had spoken."

Several months after Genevieve learned of her mother's death, she wondered if her master ever gave a second thought to her loss. Since he had only just buried his wife and now had five motherless children on his hands, did he ever stop to think how she must feel, ripped away from her mother at the age of nine, only now at sixteen learning that her mother had been dead these seven years? Did he remember reading the letter to her? Must he not have felt at least some of her loss coming so quickly after his own?

It was a sad letter and still she treasured it. After all, it was the first letter she had ever received. She often took it out to examine it, unfolding it, studying the strange, mysterious marks, and then refolding it along the same creases. The letter and the purse were all Genevieve had— the only ties to her mother and her New Orleans past— those and the scars she could feel if she rubbed her hand along her back.

Shortly after Genevieve received this letter, a new man, young, tall, good-looking, came to work for the senator. His name was James and he was born in Richmond. He had lived there until the senator had bought him for the sum of eight hundred dollars. He quickly became a jack-of-all-trades. He awoke early, made repairs, and took care of the grounds in the morning. Trained in carpentry, he spent his afternoons in the woodshed. In the evening he served dinner to the senator and his children.

But soon Genevieve became the subject of James' attentions. James would stop to pay his respects and offer to carry things for her. Late in the afternoon he could often be found talking to Genevieve in the kitchen. And on one such afternoon he presented her with his own handiwork, a beautifully constructed box out of cherry with a lid on hinges "to keep things in."

Before too long, James and Genevieve were married by a minister in the Methodist church—wed in the eyes of the Lord, but not by law. They lived with the knowledge that if their master ever chose to separate them, to sell one and not the other, he was free to do so.

Sometimes Louisa had a hard time imagining that her mother had been born free. The story of her capture and her journey to Washington sounded too horrible. But then she remembered the beautiful beaded purse her mother kept in the box her father had made. Every once in a while Genevieve would let Louisa pull it out and play with it. "When I touched the purse, that's when I knows my mother's story was not just some nightmare. It was true," Louisa told Abby.

Chapter VII
Cousin Ruthie

Louisa camped out in Abby's room for a week, eating the food Abby smuggled upstairs. As far as the two girls could tell, no one in the house suspected Louisa's presence. Word spread throughout the city that one of the fugitives had escaped from the jail. Although an officer of the law came by to question Abby's parents, he had not searched the house. Louisa had not yet been discovered, but she and Abby both worried that she might soon be detected.

Stories of the capture of the *Pearl* and the mob's reaction to it still filled the pages of the *National Era*. Abby's father denied any claim that he or others in his office had encouraged the slaves to escape or that they were in any way involved. He published a long account of the events and their aftermath, including the attempt to destroy his press: "Had we consented to remove our press, it would have been a disgrace not only to ourselves, but to the city. The fact would have gone abroad to the world that a free press could not be published in the capital city of the model republic."

Freedom of the press was a value her father held dear to his heart. He would defend this right with every breath in his body. With this freedom came a responsibility. As a man of the press he must be trusted to tell the truth. He would not lie about his actions. Abby got to thinking that her father was so concerned with the concept of freedom of the press that he had forgotten the plight of the slaves aboard the *Pearl*. She feared that in his mind the threat to the press had superseded the rights of the slaves. He had devoted much of his life to abolition—but now his head was filled with this idea that to her seemed so abstract. Did he not see that the future, indeed the very lives of the seventy-six slaves, were in danger? And if he were to stumble on Louisa in his own house, would he not reach out to her? Or would he turn her out, not because he did not care for her, but because he felt compelled to do only that of which he could speak openly? Abby knew her father would disapprove of what she was doing. He would think she was putting herself in a position where she might be forced to hide the truth. But her father would not lie. It was that simple. And that complicated.

Yet to help the slave, to allow Louisa or other slaves their rights, it might be necessary to act in secrecy. There were some deeds that could not be printed in the newspaper, even an abolitionist paper like the *National Era*. Abby's parents had taught her that her first allegiance was to God and her conscience, not to the laws of her country. If this indeed was the case, and if upholding the laws meant she had to compromise her values, then was she not making the right choice in hiding Louisa—both from the law and from her parents? Even if she had to lie?

Every night Abby would go downstairs for dinner and return with food for Louisa. On the evening of the seventh day, Abby stayed downstairs for more than an hour. Louisa grew more impatient and her stomach grumbled. She snuggled up against Charlie who was lying peacefully at the foot of the bed. She listened to his noisy breathing. "It's just you and me," she whispered. Charlie grunted without opening his eyes. Finally, Abigail burst into the room with the pockets of her pinafore bulging.

"I can't believe it took me so long to get up here. They kept asking me all these questions. But the one thing they didn't ask was why my pockets look like this. So here," Abby pulled out a roll. "And here," she said pulling out yet another roll. "And now this," she added as she drew a turkey leg out of her pocket, leaving a sizable grease stain. "You won't be hungry tonight," Abby smiled and looked up at her friend. "Louisa, why are you wearing your shawl? You can't go any place. You know that. Why, they may see you! Louisa, don't be angry with me. I got away as soon as I could," she said.

Louisa told Abby she could not stay indefinitely in her room. It was simply too confining. She could not speak above a whisper. She could not even walk around the room for fear someone would hear her footsteps. Instead, Louisa spent hours memorizing the quilt pattern on Abigail's bed. She studied the roses on the doll's china tea set that rested on a high shelf. But she was tired of picking up the fragile pieces to examine them. The first time she'd blown away the dust and trembled slightly lest she drop a piece. Now not a speck of dust remained. "I'm just not the kind of person who can stay in a room all day long waiting for minutes to pass by—even if Charlie's here to keep me company," Louisa continued. "Besides, sooner or later, one of your parents is going to get suspicious."

"But you can't just go out in the middle of the night—without a plan, without a friend," Abigail protested.

"I done it before. There ain't no reason why I can't do it again. My mind's made up. There ain't no turning back. I thank you for the rolls and I thank you for the turkey leg. They'se coming with me."

"You've got to think it over. Wait till morning," Abby pleaded, grabbing Louisa's arm.

"I made up my mind the night I set foot on the *Pearl*. I made up my mind I weren't going to be a slave no more. I knew that also meant that I had to give up my home. But I couldn't take that feeling of being owned by another person. I didn't like not making my own decisions, being told to do this, do that, go here, go there, fetch this, and don't forget that. It ain't right for a person not to be free. I do something one way, and then Missus Frye say that ain't right. I should do it another way. I don't fold the laundry the way she like. I don't clean the pots to her liking. I don't make the bed tight enough. You know, Abby, I don't see things changing. Missus Frye not goin' to change her ways. I ain't goin' to get my freedom by askin'—I just gots to take it," Louisa said, folding her arms over her chest.

Abby wanted to explain to Louisa that she could not leave without a plan. She told her, "You've got to think ahead—"

"Oh, Abby, don't you see I'se looking into the future and that's why I'm doin' what I'm doin'," Louisa answered, sitting on the bed, her head in her hands. "If I ain't never run away, it just would have been more of the same—that same feeling of being a prisoner—every day like all the other days and none of them the way I want."

Louisa thought about how much she would miss her own family when she left Washington. She couldn't expect them to follow her. Her father was quite ill. She wasn't sure he would ever recover. One of his legs was always swelling up to twice its normal size, so he always had to keep it propped up. But she wasn't going to talk about that to Abby. Not now, anyway.

A loud, booming knock suddenly resonated through the house. Louisa grabbed Abby. Both girls trembled as they heard another knock on the front door, this time louder than before. Abby tightened her clasp on Louisa's wrist. "They knows where I am. Now they'se after me," Louisa exclaimed.

"I won't let them take you. Quick—you've got to hide. Under the bed," Abby said.

"I can't hide there. That's the first place they'll look. I could jump," Louisa said looking at the window.

"Don't be silly. That's way too dangerous. You'd get hurt. Besides they might have brought dogs with them." She looked around the room. "Can you fit in the trunk?" she asked.

"But Abby, how would I breathe?" Louisa asked.

"Abby, Abby," her mother called from downstairs. "We have a visitor."

"You better go or she'll come up to get you," Louisa warned. "I'll think of something. Just go. Try not to let them come up here. Go, Abby. It will only be worse if you stay here."

Abby walked slowly downstairs planning her next move. *I'll need to make myself appear calm,* she thought. She tucked her blouse into her skirt, pulled her hair back, and pushed it behind her ears. *When I walk into the room I'll look the visitor in the eyes. If he asks about a fugitive, I'll just shake my head and say, "Why, I haven't seen anyone that meets that description."* As Abby reached the bottom step, she heard her mother laugh. If her mother knew what she knew, she wouldn't be laughing.

Abby opened the door to the drawing room. The visitor was someone she least expected.

"Cousin Ruthie!" she shouted, running towards her and giving her a big hug.

A half hour later Abby opened the door to her room, slipped in, and shut the door. "Louisa," she called softly. No answer. She lit the lamp and called again. *Surely, Louisa did not try to escape through the window.* Quickly she looked under the bed and in the wardrobe. There was no other place to look. Abby moved towards the window. *If Louisa fell, wouldn't we have heard her scream?*

Abby's heart raced as she leaned her head out the window. Turning her head to the side, she caught sight of Louisa. She was standing on the ledge—her hand clung to the branch of a tree for balance. Abby shuddered. "Louisa, you can come inside now," she called out. "Everything's going to be all right. We were wrong—it wasn't the police. No one is after you. It's my Cousin Ruthie! Here, grab my hand. You mustn't fall."

"You ain't joking now, are you?" Louisa asked.

Slowly and stealthily Louisa slid along the window ledge and climbed back inside the room. Louisa told Abby, "The next time I leave this house, I'm goin' through a door."

"Louisa, you don't know how scared I was until I saw Cousin Ruthie," Abby confided. "Then I just knew everything was going to be all right. Ruthie's able to do anything. She's the kind of person who likes to solve everybody's problems and most of the time she's pretty good at it. She's on her way back to Ohio where she teaches and she can take you with her. You can dress up in a disguise so nobody will recognize you. Ruthie could pretend you were sick and that way you wouldn't have to answer a lot of questions. If anyone asks, Ruthie will say you're traveling with her. She'll vouch for you. Lots of people make their escape that way. Don't you see this is a perfect plan? When you get to Ohio, why you're practically in Canada. You can go with Ruthie to Lake Erie. I'm sure you won't have trouble finding a boat to take you across. From what I hear people in Ohio are real helpful."

Louisa's eyes brightened and she asked, "Oh, Abby, do you think it would work?"

"We'll get you a disguise," Abigail answered. "We won't tell Mother and Father. Only Ruthie. The fewer people who know the better."

Louisa hugged her friend and said, "It sounds about as wild as most of your ideas."

"There's only one thing," Abby warned.

"What's that?" Louisa questioned.

Abby replied, "I haven't asked her yet."

Chapter VIII
Louisa's Journey

Ruthie talked so much that Louisa thought traveling with her was going to be easy. The other passengers in the stagecoach would be so busy listening to Ruthie that they wouldn't pay any attention to her. Cousin Ruthie, as Abby liked to call her, always had something to say and came across as a friendly sort of person. She was a little plump, with soft folds of skin and a round face. Dressed for traveling, she wore a new hat, decorated with feathers, and tied with silk ribbons around her rather large chin.

Louisa was disguised in trousers and a large shirt and vest. Her hair was tied back and hidden by a man's hat. Abby had taken the clothes from her brother Marcellus without asking his permission. Louisa hoped she was not causing too much trouble. Abby had assured her it would be all right. "We're only doing this because it's necessary," she told Louisa. Everyone in Washington knew one of the fugitives on the *Pearl*—a young female slave—had escaped. The senator had posted a notice offering a reward for her return. All young black girls, not in the company of their owners, would be under suspicion and expected to show a pass. If Louisa had not dressed as a boy, it was likely that she would be stopped and questioned upon boarding the stagecoach—even when escorted by the domineering Cousin Ruthie.

It wasn't until Louisa and Cousin Ruthie actually stepped onto the stagecoach that Cousin Ruthie told Louisa they weren't really headed for Ohio. Like her cousin Gamaliel, Ruthie suffered from digestive disorders. Before going back to Ohio, she wanted to take a water cure at Glenhaven, a spa in upstate New York, famous for its ice-cold springs. Ruthie had just learned that a room in the lodge had opened up. She said she hoped it was on the lake side because she always liked a room with a view. Ruthie told Louisa not to worry. She could rest at Glenhaven for a day or two and then make it safely to Niagara Falls and into Canada.

Louisa, surprised by the change in plans, but not disappointed, leaned back in her seat, folded her hands in her lap, and looked down. She wanted to appear as inconspicuous as possible in her disguise. Ruthie was rambling on about the heat and humidity in Washington. She didn't see why anyone would want to live in a swamp. She was glad to get away before the weather got much worse. Clearly, Ruthie was a person who liked to talk. That suited Louisa. She could just sit back and listen.

Louisa stole a glance at the dark-skinned man facing her. He seemed so relaxed that Louisa surmised he must be free. *Nothin' botherin' him,* Louisa thought. *If only I could act like him.*

"Whooah there!" the driver shouted with a full-throated cry. The stagecoach came to a quick, abrupt halt. The passengers in the rear lurched forward, falling against the people who sat facing them. Louisa found herself thrown next to the older black gentleman. As he looked at her closely, Louisa felt that the man could read her face. He would see the panic in her eyes and know her secret. She was apprehensive, but at the same time she felt something comforting in his knowledge. Here was someone she could trust. It was not just the color of his skin. There was something more. He would look out for her safety. She needed to relax. She gripped the seat with her hands and kept her eyes focused not on Ruthie, but on the man in the seat opposite her.

The driver stuck his head in the window of the coach. "Roadblock ahead," he announced. The man she had bumped into leaned his head towards the window and whispered to the driver. *Just like two conspirators,* Louisa thought. She could not make out their exact words, but they sounded quite agitated. The driver walked off in a great hurry.

The older black gentleman, the one she had decided to trust, turned to Louisa and said, "If you don't have papers, you're not safe here. I have one word of advice. Run." He cocked his head towards Ruthie and said, "The men who put up the roadblock are going to do a search. They'll demand to see papers." Then he almost smiled, "Talking won't help this time."

Louisa knew she had no papers, no pass to travel, and no written proof that she belonged to Cousin Ruthie. *What a fool I've been!* Louisa thought. *Did I really suppose no one would stop and question me?* She looked down at her clothes. *Do I look like a boy or do I just look like a girl in disguise?* But she had no time to think. She would have to act quickly. *If I take this man at his word, I should not delay another minute. I should just run.*

Louisa whispered to Ruthie, "I don't think I have a chance if I stay in the carriage." Her heart pounded. *If I leave now, I'm on my own. Completely.* She looked at the man who had advised her. He stared back, but did not speak. She read the message in his eyes: "Go now. Don't wait any longer. If you stay, you'll get caught. If you run, you still have hope."

Ruthie took her hand and squeezed it. "You're such a brave girl, Louisa," she said. She meant every word.

Louisa held onto her hat with one hand and opened the door with the other. Then in a flash she was gone. The light was dim and, as soon as she passed behind a tree, the passengers in the carriage lost sight of her.

She ran until she was out of breath and thought she would drop. She passed through woods where the trees were so dense that they shaded the sky from view. Only a pale light filtered through. Gradually, the light grew fainter still and the night blackened. The thick foliage blocked the stars. Without them Louisa did not know in what direction she was headed. She hoped she was pointed north, but she could not tell.

When she finally did stop to rest, she found a spot among the trees and a bed of moss for her head. Louisa could fall asleep now and know that no one would disturb her. Of course she did not know what tomorrow would bring, but for now it did not seem to matter. The trees provided all the comfort she needed. She and Abby had always wanted to camp outdoors on the banks of the Potomac, but they had never dared. The senator would never have permitted her to be absent for a night. And besides, Abby's parents were way too strict to let her go.

The morning light broke through the trees, waking Louisa from her sleep. She did not open her eyes right away, but kept them closed, trying to prolong the night and postpone the time for making a plan, coming up with a plot that would help save her life. Shutting her eyes kept her in a world that was safe.

Then suddenly a shadow threatened her security. This was not the wind making the branches sway—she could sense another person close by. The presence of another human sent fear into every pore of her body. She had to think fast. She could not afford to make a wrong move—the stakes were too high. She wanted to keep her eyes closed so as not to come face to face with her predator.

She did not want to play possum—she wanted to play dead. If this human thought she were dead, he might get scared and just leave her alone. But if he thought she were among the living, he'd wake her up and start asking all sorts of questions.

She felt a stick poke her in the ribs and then brush against her face. The tickling brought a smile to her lips even though she'd never been so scared in her life. She couldn't help opening her eyes. The first thing she noticed about the person was that he was white. The color of his skin crushed any hope of safety. The second thing that hit her was that he was a child—seven, maybe eight years old.

"You slept here—all night?" he asked, his mouth open wide, amazed that she had not spent the night in a regular bed.

"Sure did," Louisa answered.

"But you didn't have any covers," he exclaimed.

"It was a warm night."

"You mean your parents let you do that?"

Louisa paused. She could not tell her secret to a stranger even if he was just a boy. But she had never been too terribly comfortable at making up stories.

"Maybe you don't have parents," the boy said and quickly added, "I shouldn't have said that." He started drawing in the dirt with his stick. He drew a circle. Louisa, sitting up, took another stick and added two eyes. The boy drew a mouth. Louisa used her stick to draw hair. The boy started to laugh. Louisa next drew a square and the boy put in a door. They kept drawing in the dirt. Whatever Louisa did made the boy laugh.

"You're not a boy. You're a girl. I can tell," the boy said.

"You're right," Louisa answered. There no longer seemed any point in pretending. Surely this boy was not looking for the young girl who had escaped from the Washington jail.

Then the boy stopped poking in the sand and said, "I know a place where you can find berries. They're really ripe now."

"Do you want to show me?" Louisa asked. The boy took her by the hand and started down the path. He then cut across the undergrowth straight up a slope. The hill was so steep they had to grab onto vines to make their way up. The boy was true to his word. He led Louisa to a thick clump of blackberries—juicy, sweet, and plentiful. The two picked and ate until their lips turned purple.

"Do you want to come home with me?" the boy asked.

"I can't."

"You don't have to worry. I know you're running away—you're not the first to pass through here. That's why you dressed up as a boy, but you didn't fool me. You don't have to be scared. My parents will take care of you."

Louisa looked at the boy, but didn't answer. If she was going to make it to safety she would need to take help from strangers. But this was different from accepting passage on the *Pearl*. She was alone now and no one would tell her what to do or where to go. She had to make up her own mind and she had to be able to think on her feet.

"What's the matter?" the boy asked. "You got to believe me. You know we've had people like you in our house before. I'm not supposed to talk about it but we even have a secret room in our house. There's no door to it. I mean nothing that looks like a door."

Louisa knew he was too young to be making this up. She smiled and nodded. Someone out there was looking out for her. She wanted to throw her arms around this little boy and give him a great big hug. "That would be nice," she muttered instead.

Chapter IX
The Trial

Abby never told her parents about Louisa hiding in her room. She didn't want to make them angry, but it was hard having to keep her secret to herself. She kept hoping she would hear from Louisa, yet day after day passed with no word, no message. At dinner she often asked her parents if they had heard from Cousin Ruthie, but they had yet to receive a letter from her and wondered why Abby cared so much.

What her parents seemed most concerned about was the pending trial of the two captains of the *Pearl*. In fact most of Washington could talk of little else. Friends of the Baileys, Northern abolitionists, held a public meeting at Faneuil Hall in Boston to rouse public interest in assuring a fair trial. An anti-slavery committee asked an eloquent attorney and new congressman from Massachusetts, Horace Mann, to represent Daniel Drayton, the first captain to be tried. Abolitionist Samuel Gridley Howe made a special trip to Washington to convince the highly principled Mr. Mann to take the case. The congressman finally agreed to represent Captain Drayton even though it would mean spending even more time away from Massachusetts and the family he had left behind.

Mr. Mann visited Daniel in prison and explained to him that he had been charged not once, but many times. If found guilty he would be fined separately for each charge. The greater the number of charges—or indictments—the higher the fines and the more severe the penalty. The district attorney had accused the captain of "stealing, taking, and carrying away" the slaves. For this offense he received forty-one indictments, one for each of the slave-holding families who had lost their "property."

But this was not the only crime for which Daniel would be tried. The prosecution also charged him with a second crime—"transporting" the slaves and thereby assisting in their escape to freedom. The number of indictments for this crime totaled seventy-four, one for each of the seventy-four slaves from the District he had tried to transport. He would be tried later in a Virginia court for transporting the two slaves who had lived there.

As Daniel listened to Mr. Mann's account of the pending trial, he developed a nervous twitch. His upper lip started to shake uncontrollably. He envisioned months spent in his cell and worried about what would happen to his family now that he could not support them. Mr. Mann assured him that the anti-slavery committee in Boston would provide for his family. In fact, they had already sent money to the captain's wife.

For weeks the city awaited the start of the trial. Men and women of both races discussed the case on street corners and over backyard fences. Slave holders hoped for a speedy trial with a guilty verdict and a harsh sentence that would deter others from helping fugitives. They wanted retribution—the more drastic, the better. The sentence needed to send an alarm that would vibrate throughout the city.

More than three months after Captain Drayton was captured and imprisoned, on Thursday, July 27, the trial began. On that morning the jail was hot and stuffy, as it had been for weeks. The atmosphere outside offered no relief; it too was sweltering. The warden accompanied the prisoner from the jail to the courthouse. Daniel looked forward to breathing fresh air for the first time in months—the mugginess was unexpected. The clothes his jail keepers made him wear stuck to his body.

On this day Captain Drayton would be tried for stealing Andrew Houver's two slaves. But this was only the beginning. Later he would be tried for the other indictments. In addition to Horace Mann, an attorney named James Carlisle, an elderly gentleman, also eloquent and polished, was defending the captain. Philip Barton Key, the district attorney, a quite dapper gentleman, who liked to dress in cream-colored breeches and bright vests, led the prosecution.

Abigail slipped into the back of the courtroom and took a seat in the last row. A wide-brimmed bonnet hid most of her face. Abby did not want anyone to recognize her. She had to keep her presence at the trial secret. Her parents would say she was too young to be there.

Three months had passed since Abby had seen Louisa. Just before Abby had said good-bye to her friend she promised to pay close attention to the trial and write Louisa all she heard and saw. Now, she had no way of reaching Louisa, but as soon as she learned her whereabouts, she would have so much to put in her letter. She had already made long lists.

Abby watched Mr. Key rise and face the jury. Blood had rushed to his head, whether from heat or anger she was not sure. He looked positively indignant. "The right of property has been hideously violated by the man you see before you," he declared pointing to Captain Drayton with an arm that shook. "Captain Drayton arrived in Washington on a Monday," he said. "He did not leave again until Saturday. What caused this delay? Why did he choose not to return sooner? Did he have other business to take care of in Washington? He had no business of which I am aware—except that of enticing slaves to board his ship. Once the slaves had safely boarded, Captain Drayton could take them where he pleased. Indeed, we will show that he intended to sail to the Caribbean and sell the slaves for a huge profit. For this crime, for luring the slaves onto the

Pearl with the intent to sell them, this prisoner must be convicted," he stated, tapping his fist on the railing for emphasis.

Abby could not believe what she was hearing. *Surely Captain Drayton did not want to steal the slaves. It's ridiculous to assume he lured the slaves onto the boat with the intent to sell them. Mr. Key is unfairly accusing him of a major crime. Does Mr. Key really think Captain Drayton planned to sell them or is this just a trick to turn the jury against the captain?*

The district attorney would not rest with one accusation. He fought to prove that Captain Drayton was guilty not only of stealing the slaves with the intent of selling them, but also of transporting them to assist in their escape. Abby did not understand how Mr. Key thought he could accuse Mr. Drayton of two such different crimes. *Either he planned to steal them or he planned to help them escape. He could not do both. If he is to be found guilty of one crime, he cannot be guilty of the other.* It just didn't make any sense to her.

A guilty verdict for either crime would result in a severe penalty. Abby knew the punishment for stealing a slave called for "confinement in the penitentiary for not less than twenty years." Another law provided that any person who assisted in the transporting of a slave "by advice, donation or loan, or otherwise" would be fined a sum "not exceeding $200, at the discretion of the court."

Abby quickly calculated that if you multiplied $200 by
seventy-four, the number of slaves from the District aboard
the *Pearl*, the fine would be preposterous. If he were found
guilty of this offense, Captain Drayton would owe $14,800.
How could he ever raise that much money?

Mr. Key called to the stand Andrew Houver, a white-
haired man who stooped as he walked. Mr. Houver put
one hand on the Bible and looked straight into the eyes of
the bailiff as he was sworn in. "Drayton meant to steal
my two slaves," Mr. Houver testified. "That man," he said,
pointing to Captain Drayton, "wanted to sail the *Pearl* to
the West Indies and then sell the slaves who rightfully
belong to me." For proof Mr. Houver claimed that enough
food to last a month had been found on the boat. "Let me
ask you, why would this captain need so many provisions
were he only going to New Jersey?" Mr. Houver raised his
eyebrows, pursed his lips, and nodded his head as if to
say that any man, not half as old or wise as he, could
easily deduce the answer.

"Tell me," Mr. Mann said in cross-examination, "have
you ever taken it upon yourself to obtain food for a group
that size?"

"I have not," Mr. Houver answered. "I'm afraid I don't
find myself in that line of work." One of the jurymen
laughed and the man next to him poked him with his elbow.

"Perhaps you would like to tell us again exactly what
provisions were found aboard the *Pearl* and explain to us

how you would use them to feed eighty for a one-month period," Mr. Mann replied.

Mr. Houver was forced to admit he had reached a stumbling block. After further questioning, he conceded that the provisions the *Pearl* carried would not last more than a few days, let alone a month.

It was now Mr. Mann's turn to present his argument. Although he may have scored a point with the last witness, Mr. Mann knew the crowd was hostile. Many of those now present in the courtroom were the same ones who had gathered at the dock when the *Salem* returned with the *Pearl* in tow. They had jeered at Captain Drayton, shouted "Hang him!" and "Lynch him!" and threatened him with knives. Present too was the man who had sliced off a portion of Captain Drayton's ear. Mr. Mann's duty was to win them to his side. He appealed to the court to let the captain have a fair trial.

Mr. Mann explained that a man named David Bell had first approached Captain Drayton with a plea to help his family escape. The father of eight children, David had worked hard to earn enough money to buy his own freedom. After many years he succeeded. His master told him that in his final will he would grant David's wife and children their freedom. Yet upon his death, the master's heirs claimed that the master was not of sound mind when he made his last will. The Bells feared the court would rule against them and therefore determined their best course would be to flee north. David got word to Captain Drayton that he was looking for someone to rescue his wife and children.

Although Captain Drayton wanted to oblige, he had lost his oyster boat in foul weather. He told David he could not help him. However, a few weeks later David pressed him again. This time Captain Drayton agreed to inquire about hiring a boat. In Frenchtown, New Jersey, he convinced Edward Sayres, the captain of a boat called the *Pearl*, to sail down to Washington, pick up the Bell family, and then return to Frenchtown. They would carry a load of timber—twenty cords of wood—for delivery to Washington as a cover for their real mission.

When they arrived in Washington on Thursday, April 13, word of Captain Drayton's plot spread. Within forty-eight hours the number of slaves who planned to escape far exceeded the captain's expectations.

"It is a case which, in some of its aspects, touches the deepest and tenderest sympathies of the human heart," said Mr. Mann, "for this prosecution not only deals with human beings as offenders, but with human beings and human rights, as the subject matters of the offense."

Mr. Mann then challenged the notion of accusing the defendant of two separate crimes. "If the prisoner stole the slaves, he is not guilty of the separate offense of transporting. If he is guilty of transporting, he is not guilty of stealing. That the two offenses should have been committed by one and the same act is a legal impossibility," Mr. Mann declared. "Not only is he accused of two crimes, but he has received one hundred fifteen separate indictments— seventy-four indictments for transporting (one for each slave in question) and forty-one indictments for stealing (one for each slave-holder who lost one or more slaves). Now I ask this court: What purpose is served by such a great number of indictments? Who can survive a contest against such a host of indictments, sustained by all the power and resources of the government?" Mr. Mann asked.

"The dirty scoundrel!" one of the men in the front row shouted.

Ignoring him, Mr. Mann continued, "Gentlemen, I maintain that what may be proved against the defendant is at the most the offense of transportation, but not of stealing."

With a quick glance around the courtroom, Mr. Mann saw that he commanded the complete attention of his audience. "We all know that many blacks can read. Who knows but some of them have read the Declaration of American Independence and applied its immortal truths to themselves. 'All men are created equal and among their inalienable rights are life, LIBERTY, and the pursuit of happiness!' Those who cannot read can hear."

Mr. Mann paused and stepped closer to the jury. "I entreat you to think back a moment. Remember the day the *Pearl* first arrived in our fair city. Was not there a torchlight procession and a feeling of great joy that overtook our capital? People reveled in the streets, sang praises to liberty, and rejoiced in the new-found freedom of the French people. Music was played and bonfires blazed. Many colored lanterns graced our avenues and the house of the president was illuminated. People of all kinds and colors gathered on Pennsylvania Avenue to hear speeches from our senators. And on what subject did they speak? Why liberty, of course. And did not one of them declare that the age of TYRANTS AND SLAVERY is rapidly drawing to a close? I ask you—Would not slaves who came to hear these words be swayed to seek their own liberty?"

Judge Thomas Crawford, his face scarlet, interrupted Mr. Mann, "The court thinks it must interfere and ask the counsel not to use such inflammatory language."

Mr. Carlisle then rose to explain that his partner Mr. Mann had only wished to convey that the slaves in all likelihood had heard the speeches given that night and would have been inspired to gain their freedom.

District Attorney Philip Barton Key stood and, turning towards Mr. Mann, demanded, "Who gave this speech? How do we know these are the words that were spoken?"

"I read the words of a speech given by Senator Henry Foote of Mississippi from the April 20 issue of the *Washington Union*," Mr. Mann said looking squarely at his adversary. He could see the tiny beads of perspiration on Mr. Key's forehead.

"But what proof do you have that he spoke these words?" Mr. Key asked.

"If you like, we can call Senator Foote to the stand," Mr. Mann replied.

"We all know the senator was not referring to slaves when he spoke of these principles," the judge said, hoping to bring a close to the discussion.

Mr. Mann faced the jury. The jurymen kept their eyes cast down. Mr. Mann was determined to have the last word: "I wish only to say that these words could incite a slave to leave his master. This speech, and others like it, may have influenced Mr. Houver's slaves, although I am quite sure that throughout their lives they frequently thought and dreamt of liberty. Their decision to leave their master cannot be reduced to a single event nor a single speech. If we could we would call these slaves to the stand as witnesses and we could hear from them why they left in the dark of the night. But the law shuts up their mouths."

How utterly foolish, Abby thought, *that the slaves by law cannot testify. How can anyone sitting in this courtroom not be horrified by such an absurd law?* One of the jury members, a young man, fair skinned with reddish cheeks, now visibly upset, grabbed the sides of his chair. Abby wondered whether he was angered by the silence imposed on the slaves or threatened by the suggestion that they be allowed to speak.

Removing a handkerchief from his pocket, Mr. Mann wiped his brow, and said, "No evidence that the prisoner planned to use the services of the slaves or to sell them can be found." Here Mr. Mann paused and then added, "Because there is none."

For his first witness Mr. Mann called forward a sailor, Thomas Rutherford, who had watched the *Pearl* return to Washington. He had boarded the *Pearl* "to get a look around" after the slaves were led off the ship. "Nobody paid me no mind. The crowd had their eyes on the slaves."

"Thank you, Mr. Rutherford. And while you were aboard the *Pearl*, did you form an opinion as to the condition of the boat?" Mr. Mann interjected.

"If you ask me—and you did—I'd tell you that the *Pearl* is a mere bay-craft and cannot be taken safely to sea on a long journey. No sailor of sound mind would take the *Pearl* to the Caribbean," he stated emphatically.

Mr. Mann then called his next witness, an acquaintance of Captain Drayton from Philadelphia, and asked if he had ever heard the captain talk about helping a black man reach a free state. The man answered, "I don't know whether he done it or not. But he sure did talk about it."

Mr. Key cross-examined him, "Do you not think Captain Drayton was just like the other watermen who bragged of running off slaves?"

"These watermen talk a big game, but if they dare to take a slave on board, they ain't thinking about profit," the witness answered. "They're just aimin' to help a fellow out."

After Mr. Mann asked the witness to step down, his partner, James Carlisle, recovering from gout and still frail, summoned all his strength to issue a strong warning to the jury: "It is your duty to go into the examination of this novel case carefully and to take care that no man and no court shall be able to say that your verdict is not warranted by the evidence. If the case is made out against the prisoner, convict him; but if not, as you value the reputation of the District and your own souls, beware how you give a verdict against him!" He reminded the jury that the eyes of the world were watching. "God forbid that the world should point to this trial as a proof that we are so besotted by passion and interest that we cannot discern the most obvious distinctions and that on a slave question with a jury of slave holders there is no possible chance of justice!"

The jury was dismissed. Abby would have to wait until the next day to hear the verdict. A long night lay ahead. If only she could tell Louisa what was happening.

Chapter X
The False-Bottomed Wagon

At first Louisa counted every day she spent with the boy's family. Once she got to fourteen, the days started to blur together and she lost track. Every evening she went to bed with her stomach full. Zach's mother kept putting more on her plate so that it never appeared empty. Louisa couldn't bear to turn her down. The Harwood family's hospitality was a new experience. But she wasn't going to stay with this family forever and she couldn't help thinking that each day might be her last in the Harwood home.

In the meantime she would enjoy her own "secret" room adjacent to Zach's bedroom, a hideaway designed to fool slave catchers. From Zach's side you could not notice the door into her room. Only if you examined the wall paneling closely could you see a slightly recessed area. If you applied pressure there, the panel slid to the left, creating an opening into the room that was now hers.

No one had ever showered her with so much attention or made her feel quite so special. Whenever she visited the Baileys, Abby's mother had always been nice to her, but didn't spoil her. And from the time she turned twelve until the day she boarded the *Pearl,* she had never spent more than a day away from Mrs. Frye. That meant she was constantly subject to her whims and commands. Of course at the Bailey house, after she escaped, Abby was looking out for her, but she didn't exactly feel like an honored guest. She had to remember to whisper and to tread lightly on the floor so no one would hear. Living secretly at the Baileys was somewhat akin to leading the life of a captive.

One morning, after Louisa had grown accustomed to the new routine in Zach's house, she awoke in a room filled with bright sunlight. She had overslept. She jumped out of bed, dressed hurriedly, and slid open the secret panel on the hidden door. Stepping downstairs, she smelled sausage cooking in the kitchen below. Her mouth started to water. *Another day and still not caught,* she thought. And what's more she still hadn't gone hungry. When she sat down at the table, Elizabeth, Zach's mother, put a bowl of porridge in front of her. Standing over the stove, her forehead moist from the steam, she said, "Enjoy your breakfast, Louisa. I made your favorite biscuits. They're pipin' hot."

Louisa sat at her place at the table and stuck her napkin under her chin. She watched as Elizabeth ladled gravy over her biscuits.

"I have something to tell you," Elizabeth said. Her voice sounded much like her own mother when she wanted

Louisa's full attention and was about to discuss something serious like her father's illness.

"I'm listening," Louisa said, meaning that she would brace herself to hear something she didn't want to hear.

"You know that Hugh is worried about your safety," Elizabeth began. She explained that the capture of the *Pearl* had caused a furor in Washington. The slave holders were outraged that so many slaves had tried to escape. They lived in fear that a second attempt would be made and they vowed to stop at nothing to punish the fugitives. Most were sold to slave traders and sent to New Orleans to be auctioned. Word of the young female slave's escape, however, had spread. Notices offering a reward for her capture were posted around the capital and distributed throughout Maryland and Delaware.

"If you remain in this area, you risk capture by slave hunters," Elizabeth warned her. Louisa had stopped eating. Elizabeth's voice became more soothing as she continued, "You mustn't despair. You simply need to recognize that the situation is serious. We have some good news for you. We've gotten word that an older couple, a good couple, are preparing to sail to England—"

"England!" Louisa almost shouted. *What is Elizabeth saying? Why is she talking about safety? Ain't I safe with Elizabeth, Hugh, and Zach? Why can't I stay with them? Here we are in the middle of nowhere. Who's goin' to find me here? Everything's been goin' so well. Why must things change?* But no sooner had these questions flown into her head than she started thinking how presumptuous she was. The Harwoods had gotten along fine before she'd tumbled into their lives. Still, she didn't know quite what to say.

Elizabeth continued, "You're awfully quiet this morning. Now I need to tell you about this couple. Samuel was freed when his master died and then shortly afterwards bought his wife's freedom. They're hoping they can raise more money in London to buy freedom for other slaves. They know you've made it this far and they're willing to see that you get the rest of the way. They're an older couple with no children to call their own. Hugh met them at the anti-slavery fair last summer and he went into Philadelphia yesterday to discuss your situation. They were more than eager to help. It's a wonderful offer."

Louisa took a bite from her biscuit, but had difficulty swallowing.

"You're still not talking," Elizabeth said. "I just want you to know that we're thinking about your safety. If you stay around here you'll always be looking over your shoulder. You're just too young to lead a life in hiding. You'll never be sure whether or not someone will come after you. Your escape has not gone un-noticed. You are celebrated in certain circles, but others are out to get you. If the wrong person learns you were aboard the *Pearl* you could be kidnapped, taken south, and then sold. You have no papers, nothing to show you're free."

Zach stood up and walked out of the kitchen. He left his uneaten breakfast on the table. Elizabeth called after him, but he did not answer. She turned to Louisa and said, "He's really taken to you, I think. You know he looks up to you and he just doesn't want to think about your leaving. He also doesn't want to hear that you might get in trouble somewhere down the road."

"I'll talk to him," Louisa assured her. "See if I can explain. I know you just want to look out for me."

"You've been so wonderful to Zach. I wish he didn't have to lose you," Elizabeth answered.

A week later Louisa went to bed for the last time in the room that she had come to think of as hers. She did not blow out her candle right away. She loved lying on her back and staring straight ahead at the wallpaper. There on the wall a man, dressed in what she imagined must be the height of European fashion—a shirt with a ruffle down the middle, pantaloons that flared but were drawn tight under the knee, a coat that added breadth to his shoulders, a hat with a brim, and shoes with a buckle, stood under a tree, his arm extended as he pushed a young lady on a swing. The girl was wearing fancy clothes, a dress with a tight bodice, and a long, flowing skirt. Wavy locks of hair appeared under her bonnet. On the ground, not far from the swing, lay her parasol. A walking stick, no doubt belonging to the gentleman, was leaning against the tree. *This picture must be reproduced hundreds of times*, Louisa thought, still examining the wallpaper. She could imagine herself as the young lady on the swing and she could feel the weight of the man's hand pressing on her back as he pushed her back and forth.

Part of Louisa never wanted to leave this room. She was warm, well-fed, safe. Little else mattered. But, ever since Elizabeth had told her about the plan, she had come to realize she could not stay a prisoner to this house and the Harwood hospitality. She needed to find a community where the senator and Mrs. Frye would never find her and she would not need to hide. She was only a guest at the Harwoods, not a member of the family. She would move on. The Harwoods would have many more guests, just as they had many guests before her. Louisa knew her bed would soon be occupied by another slave, on the run, seeking freedom too.

Surely she was one of the lucky ones. Tomorrow, if all went well, Zach and his father would take her to Philadelphia in their cart. The horses were in excellent shape. Hugh maintained that they could make the trip in four hours. But they would need to make an early start and leave before dawn. The wagon was equipped with a false bottom, underneath which was constructed a compartment large enough for a person to lie down in. Hugh had transported many slaves in this manner. Each journey had been a success. Anyone who passed Hugh on the road saw only a wagon loaded with timber and had no clue that underneath the "bottom" of the wagon lay a person. Louisa hoped she wouldn't have any trouble lying still for four hours. And then just think—this mysterious couple ready to take her to England.

Louisa would meet Bernice and Samuel in Philadelphia. Together they would board the steamship and make the fourteen-day trip to Liverpool. Never in her wildest dreams had she thought she would make a transatlantic voyage. Elizabeth had told her an abolitionist group in Philadelphia, the Vigilance Committee, would pay for her ticket. *How can one person have such good fortune?* Louisa wondered. *Will people in England really be dressed like the characters in the wallpaper? Do they live in beautiful houses surrounded by gardens blooming with color? Do they spend their days on a swing in a garden or riding horses with dogs running alongside?*

At five the next morning, Louisa hugged Elizabeth good-bye and squeezed into the wagon's hidden compartment. The floor of the wagon was covered with straw which made her new "bed" a little softer, but still scratchy. Zach stuck his head in and made a ghostlike sound. "You don't scare me," Louisa said.

"Out of the way now, son," Hugh said and, taking a board, placed it along the back of the wagon to close off the entrance to the secret compartment. Zach held it in place and Hugh hammered it shut. Hugh then kissed his wife on the forehead, saying good-bye. Louisa could hear

Elizabeth say, "Take care of her, Hugh. She's a mighty fine girl."

Hugh and Zach hoisted themselves up to the driver's seat and once more waved good-bye. Hugh gently prodded the horse with his whip. Then they were off. Louisa reclined on the straw, bouncing up and down, as the horse trotted forward. She had only the clothes on her back to call her own and in her pocket a present from Zach, a drawing he had made the night before of a boy and girl. It reminded her of the first time she met him when they used sticks to draw in the sand. To think that a chance encounter in the woods might lead her all the way to England.

Chapter XI
The Verdict

The night before the verdict was to be announced, Abby lay in bed watching the curtains as they blew away from the window, billowing out, balloon-shaped. The breeze was a welcome relief to the hot and muggy day. Still she could not sleep. Part of her wished Louisa hadn't left. She longed to talk to her about the trial.

As much as she wanted Louisa to stay in Washington, she understood why Louisa had chosen to run away. And yet what courage it must have taken to leave behind family and friends, no matter how great the pull of liberty. It was so hard for Abby to imagine moving away from her parents and all her sisters and brothers. And Charlie. She didn't want to think what it would be like never to see any of them again.

If only Abby could have gone along on the stagecoach with Cousin Ruthie. It worried her that she had yet to receive a letter from Cousin Ruthie and knew nothing of Louisa's whereabouts.

Maybe if she went downstairs and fixed herself a glass of milk and something sweet to eat, she would feel better. She would get her mind off her worries and she could get some rest. She hated not being able to sleep. Abby pulled off the covers, slid out of bed, and tiptoed to the door. She opened the door slowly and, careful not to make any noise, crept out of her room. The last thing she wanted was for her mother to call out, "Are you all right?"

Once downstairs she was surprised to see the light on in the library. It was her father, and not her mother, who called out, "Is that you, Abby?"

"Father, what are you doing up in the middle of the night?" Abby asked as she walked into the room.

"Thought I recognized your step on the stairs," he answered. He was still in the clothes he wore to the newspaper, his shirtsleeves rolled up, gray-checkered trousers, and a waistcoat.

"I couldn't sleep. It's just too hot," Abby explained. "I'd like to go jump in the river. That's what I'd like."

"Come here, little girl," said her father. Abby crossed over to his chair and put her arms around her father's neck. Tonight she didn't mind if he called her "little girl." He pulled her into his lap and she snuggled up against him. It had been a long time since she'd sat on his lap. She liked feeling cozy and knowing he would take care of her. Of course there were still so many things she couldn't talk to him about. Her father had a temper and she didn't want to set it off. She couldn't imagine telling him about Louisa hiding in her room or sneaking off to the trial.

Those were just things he was better off not knowing. Sometimes it bothered her that she was keeping this enormous secret from her parents. But for right now none of that mattered. She was content to have her father hold her and she didn't have to get all bothered about her secrets. She wasn't going to worry about his finding out, not now. She was sure he wouldn't ask her all sorts of questions. He knew better than to do that in the middle of the night. She rested her head on his shoulder and after a while, her father, still keeping his arm around her, opened his book and started reading. Abby read a paragraph or two, something by Thomas Carlyle, and then closed her eyes.

The next day the townspeople packed the courthouse. By the time Abby entered, the room was full, but she found a seat in the back row. Once again she did her best not to draw attention to herself, so that word of her presence would not reach her father. She had not wanted to anger him, and yet she could not stay away. She wanted to hear firsthand what happened. She felt she owed it to Louisa.

Abby waited, but the jury still did not return. The spectators grew more and more agitated. Abby watched a fly land on the head of the man in front of her. The man tried to swat the fly and missed. She listened to the conversation between the two women sitting next to her, the vivacious Ellen Swan and the elderly Cora Sands. Both women had a special interest in the trial since they counted their own slaves among the captives of the *Pearl*.

Whenever Abby saw them on the street, they would always walk right past her without saying hello. Abby wasn't too surprised by this. Her mother had explained that when the Baileys first moved to Washington from Cincinnati their reputation preceded them. Neighbors with abolitionist leanings were more than hospitable, but many others wanted nothing to do with a rabble-rouser abolitionist. They did not think twice about calling Dr. Bailey an "evil-minded abolitionist" right within earshot of Abby and her brothers and sisters.

The mayor, Colonel Seaton, and his wife proved an exception. Even a few others, who were not abolitionists, came to see that Gamaliel Bailey was a thoughtful and determined gentleman. If they bumped into Mrs. Bailey on the street, they might discuss their children's music teachers or the latest British fashions, but they cautiously avoided any talk of the newspaper or slavery.

Mrs. Swan, however, was not among those who had become civil to Mrs. Bailey, and she continued to snub her. Cora Sands did the same whenever she was with Mrs. Swan. But by herself, Mrs. Sands could manage a smile and a "how-do-you-do." On this particular day in court, Mrs. Swan and Mrs. Sands were not about to have anything to do with Abigail.

"Why, Daniel Drayton deserves to spend each of his remaining days in the penitentiary. And if he never sees the light of day, Washington will be better off for it," Mrs. Swan said to her friend, speaking loudly to ensure that everyone could overhear her.

"He ought to repent for his sins right here in jail, I should think," said Mrs. Sands.

"I didn't think Mary Hale would ever leave me. I thought she was happy," Mrs. Swan explained. "Sometimes I treated her like a sister. I even let her wear my clothes. When the Clarks sold Frank, I knew it was hard on her, but I thought she got over it. I never imagined she'd try anything so foolish. I just don't know what came over her. I didn't let her go hungry. She only worked a half-day on Sunday...," Mrs. Swan kept on talking.

Abby listened to every word without looking directly at the two women. She stared at the man's head in front of her and sometimes looked down at her hands folded on her lap. *What would Louisa say if she could hear Mrs. Swan now?*

Finally, after what seemed like hours, the door to the antechamber opened and the members of the jury filed in silently. The entire courtroom immediately grew still; no one talked or whispered; the shuffling of feet and the rustling of paper fans came to an abrupt halt. Only the flies refused to show any respect. Abby stopped swinging her feet back and forth and did not bother to brush back the lock of hair that fell into her face. She kept her eyes on the judge as he walked past the jury and took his seat. His face impassive, he asked the jury for their verdict.

"Guilty," the foreman announced. He cast his eyes down and spoke solemnly with neither pleasure nor regret. Then the man's barely perceptible thin sliver of a smile turned to a broad grin.

Judge Crawford sentenced Daniel Drayton to twenty years in the penitentiary for stealing Andrew Houver's two slaves. Abby felt the tears well up in her eyes and listened aghast as the man next to her cheered, flinging his arms wildly above his head. She looked past him at Captain Drayton. His back was slumped; his head hung low.

Chapter XII
Louisa at Sea

Louisa followed Bernice and Samuel up the gangplank at the Philadelphia pier, onto the wooden steamship that would take them all the way to Liverpool. Samuel told her the large vessel stretched over two hundred thirty feet from the tip of her pointed bow to the stern. Although one of the first ships powered by a steam engine, she was also equipped with three tall masts. Louisa could hardly believe she was standing on the deck of such a grand ship. She had never laid eyes on a ship this size, for nothing of this magnitude had ever docked at a Washington harbor. She examined the wood, shiny polished oak, the freshly painted railing, the ropes, properly knotted, neatly arranged, each in its place, and the tall smokestacks. She watched the rippling water below and the waves glistening under the sun. A gentle breeze caught her hair. Her heart pounded in anticipation.

Carrying one of Bernice and Samuel's bags, Louisa thought to herself, *I look just like a regular passenger now. Well, it's not that I don't stand out at all, but at least I could pass for a free black, not a stowaway.* She had no baggage or clothes she could call her own, but still Bernice was very good about lending her things. They were close in size although Bernice was neither quite as tall nor as thin as Louisa. Like Bernice, Louisa was dressed in a neatly pressed blouse and a long, full skirt. Bernice wrapped a long cape over her shoulders, and Louisa wore the black shawl her mother had given her. Samuel's black coat, gray trousers, and broad-brimmed hat gave him an air of distinction. Anyone watching the trio board the boat would have thought they looked much too confident to arouse suspicion, or so Louisa hoped.

"Hold it!" came a man's voice, loud and clear.

Louisa turned and saw an officer on shore wielding a gun and sprinting towards the ship. She quickly grabbed Bernice by the arm and squeezed her tightly. Once again she was about to lose the freedom that was almost hers. She had been way too self-assured. Slipping onto the boat was not going to be as easy as she had hoped. *Now I'm going to get caught,* she thought. Even here in a free state this officer could find some excuse to arrest her. The promise of a reward could turn the best-intentioned man against her. Her escape had been too bold, too daring. It was brazen to expect to board a ship in broad daylight and sail to free territory in England. *How could I think Bernice and Samuel would offer real protection?*

Then, suddenly, the officer ran onto the gangplank. He paid scant attention to her, instead dashing by her, and in his haste brushing her shoulder.

"Stop. Don't move or I'll shoot," the officer shouted as he boarded the ship. He had his back to Louisa. He was shouting not to her but to someone else.

Louisa caught a glimpse of the young man the officer was chasing. The dark-skinned fugitive sprinted with lightning speed across the top deck. He did not look back, but kept going until he came head to head with the bow of the boat. Louisa watched him climb to the top of the bow.

"This is it," the officer yelled to him. "Down on deck. You won't get another chance. I'm telling you I'm prepared to shoot."

Louisa looked up at the young man as he stood poised on the bow. He did not move. The other passengers already on board had become immobile, their heads cocked towards the sky, their eyes on the black man. Mere seconds passed, but ones that would be forever ingrained in the minds of those who watched the frozen images and listened to the eerie silence, for those seconds signified hope—hope for the freedom this man had come so close to attaining, and yet now was doomed to lose. Louisa felt a surge of sudden mixed emotions, pride in the man for not yielding, and, at the same time, trepidation for his future.

Later, Louisa would not be able to say what happened first. Was it the vision of the body leaping into the air, trying to reach the boat anchored next to theirs? Or was it the deafening sound of the gunshot breaking the silence—sharp and unmistakable?

The body made a crashing sound as, missing the boat, it landed in the water. The passengers on deck started to move closer, but the officer, still brandishing his gun, made a motion with his hand to hold them back. Louisa, clasping Bernice, shuddered. Samuel put his hand on her shoulder and squeezed it. "Shot in the back," he declared solemnly.

"I'm not so sure," Bernice answered. Louisa wondered why Bernice would question what they had just seen.

Those passengers nearest the railing searched the water for a ripple, anything, some sign of the man's presence. They looked down at the water, expecting the body to surface. The man must be wounded, but, surely, he would be alive. They studied the shoreline. *It might be possible for someone to make it to shore without taking a breath, but, once on shore, then what?* Louisa wondered. *What future for a man running from the law? What future for a black man chased by a white man with a gun at his back?*

A day later Louisa stood by the ship's railing and watched the foam combing the tips of the waves. Water was everywhere. She was a prisoner to this boat, and yet, for the first time in her life, she felt totally free. Once before she had stood by the railing on a boat, looking out to sea. She had thought then she was on her way to freedom, but, of course, she had been proven wrong. That was only the dress rehearsal. Things were different now. She did not have to remain below, crowded into a tiny space, hiding out, afraid to go on deck. She had heard stories of stowaways arriving in England inside a shipping crate, but this time she was one of the lucky ones. Now she could roam about as she pleased for everyone assumed she was free—the daughter of two free blacks. And Bernice and Samuel said things would only get better. They kept telling her, "Wait until you get to England. When you visit people, you won't have to enter through a back door. You'll march right in through the front."

Bernice and Samuel made it sound like a fairy tale. But it was not a perfect fairy tale. At one moment Louisa felt blessed with a new set of adopted parents. But the next moment she would think herself a traitor to her own mother and father. How could she put an ocean between herself and them? She would remind herself that they had wanted her to leave. "You're young. You have your whole life ahead of you," her mother said. How many times had she heard that? Her mother after all had not been taken into slavery until the age of nine. She had tasted freedom. And though she would not come right out and tell her to run, nevertheless she made it clear that she would approve. If her mother had been faced with the same choices, she too would have been on this boat heading for Liverpool. "Don't think twice. You'se doin' the right thing." That's what her mother would say.

Louisa thought of the grandparents she had never known. On her mother's side there was Marc Brodin, a white man, and Lizzie, the slave he took as a mistress, who became as dear to him as any wife. Her father knew little of his own parents. Sold at the age of four, he had rarely seen his mother though she lived less than twenty miles away from him. Although Louisa had never laid eyes on her grandparents, she could not help but think they would understand the choice she made and wish her well on her journey. It was their blood coursing through her veins that gave her the courage to flee.

Bernice and Samuel treated Louisa as one of their own in private as well as public. She knew that someone up there was looking out for her. How else to explain the wondrous good fortune that had befallen her? Louisa had adapted quickly to her new role. The trouble was that it was fun to pretend she had this new identity. She wondered if she should let herself enjoy this new life.

Abby would have a hard time believing I'm on my way to England, Louisa mused. *She thinks I'm headed for the Great Lakes, not the Atlantic Ocean.* Her friend had been so sure their first plan would work. Louisa would have to find a way to get word to Abby. Once she got to England she was bound to meet someone headed back to Washington. The Baileys frequently entertained British guests. It would not be hard to find a traveler to deliver a letter to Abby.

Of course that depended on her arriving on British shores safely and in one piece. Right now she had better lie down in her cabin before her stomach started to feel worse. The food served on the ship looked quite good and there was always plenty of it, but she had hardly been able to hold down any food for two days and was weak from hunger. She headed back towards the passenger cabins.

Walking along the narrow passageway, she heard a muffled, yet distinctly audible cough come from inside a closed door. Louisa paused by the door and heard the cough repeated. Smoky vapors escaped from the crack below the door. She must be near the boiler room where the coal was kept. On an impulse she turned the knob. Fumes and dust made it difficult to see and breathe, but the sound of another cough drew her attention to a body lying on the floor. His color was the same as her own, his eyes thin slits barely open, his forehead drenched in sweat, his shirt torn. He looked so familiar—she was sure she had seen him before. Then she knew. Here was the young man who had jumped from the bow.

The fugitive was wedged into such a confined space that he could not turn his body. He looked at Louisa, but said not a word. With her hand Louisa shielded her mouth and nose from the fumes and, bending down, asked the stranger, "Are you all right?" *That's a silly question,* she said to herself. *He's obviously in terrible pain.* She spoke softly, "Don't worry. Your secret's safe with me."

"Thank you," he answered.

"You need some water. I'll get you some," she said as she closed the door and, leaving the fumes behind, took a deep breath of sea air.

Louisa found a cup of water and returned to the boiler room. She started to hand the stowaway the cup, but when he made no effort to take it, she lifted it to his lips. *He has less strength than I thought.* He managed to halfway smile and a little water dribbled down onto his unshaven chin.

"Are you free?" he asked.

"They think I am," she answered. "Has anyone seen you here?"

"No, I don't think so," he replied. "One of the shipmates came in but he didn't say anything. It was dark. I don't think he saw me."

"I saw you fall into the water," Louisa told him. "I thought you'd been shot. I didn't think you'd—" She didn't finish her sentence.

"It's me, all right. Name's Roy. What's yours?" he asked.

"Louisa," she answered smiling. "How'd you get here? I just didn't expect to find you. I thought you—" Once again Louisa stopped herself from finishing her sentence.

"Go ahead, say it. You thought I was at the bottom of the river."

Roy told her that after he landed in the water, he stayed under as long as he could, then swam close to the bow, and grabbed hold of the barnacles attached to the side of the ship. Terrified of getting caught, he kept underwater as much as possible. He raised his head up only when he had to breathe. When the ship set sail, he was still hanging on for dear life. Only when it grew dark did he dare attempt to climb up the side of the boat and hoist himself on board.

Like me, he's run away, Louisa thought to herself. *Now there are two of us.*

She looked at Roy and saw how enormously difficult it was for him to breathe. "It's mighty hot in here. I don't know how you stand it," she blurted out.

"You'd be surprised how fast you can get used to something if you know it won't last too long and if you know you're going to like what comes after," he said.

"Shh," Louisa answered. "Don't talk so much. You'se going to wear yourself out. We just got to get you out of this room. You gonna suffocate in here. As long as you and me don't get caught, everything's goin' to turn out fine."

Chapter XIII
Blindman's Bluff

Abby jumped out of bed and pulled on a dark blue dress that she thought would make her look older, but not too conspicuous. This was one day when she did not want to stand out. She hurried downstairs and helped herself to the buckwheat cakes on the table.

"You're up early," her mother said.

"Am I? Well, it must be the change in weather," Abby answered.

Her father put his paper down and pulled his watch chain out of his pocket. He looked at her across the table. A dip in the temperature was not likely to bother Abby and her father knew it.

"Margaret, will you pass the honey please?" he asked.

Abby was relieved to find her father was not going to question her on what she was doing after school. She did not want him to tell her one more time to stay away from the courthouse. "There might be a riot and I don't want you to get hurt" was sure to be on the tip of his tongue. But her father did not speak and silently ate a bite of pancake.

111

"The Edmondson girls have returned to Alexandria," her mother said.

"You mean Emily and Mary? What happened?" Abby asked.

"The slave trader took them down to New Orleans. Thought he could make twice as much if he sold them there. But as soon as they arrived, they heard that yellow fever was sweeping the city. They say hundreds there have died. They had to send everyone who wasn't sold back up here. Bruin and Hill are keeping them locked up in Alexandria. It's a good thing your friend Louisa managed to get away."

Hearing her mother talk about Louisa made Abby nervous.

"Abigail, you're not chewing your food. You mustn't eat so quickly. It's bad for your digestion," her mother said. Why did her mother worry so much about her digestion? Her father was the one with stomach problems.

"We just have to pray that Louisa is in good hands and that she doesn't get caught," Margaret added.

Abby ate another mouthful and tried to take her time chewing. When she finished the bite, she left the table and picked up her satchel. "I'll be leaving now," she called out.

"Don't be late for school," her mother answered. It was her mother's way of saying good-bye.

Abigail closed the door behind her and crossed the street. It was a beautiful fall day. The leaves were turning and the air was crisp. Everywhere Abby looked she saw splashes of color, brilliant reds, oranges, and yellows. At the corner she turned left, not towards school, but in the direction of the courthouse. If she went to school, she would not be able to sit still. All she could think about was Captain Drayton's trial. His case had been retried after appeal and the new verdict was expected today. She wasn't going to miss that.

Horace Mann and his partner, James Carlisle, were once again disputing the notion that Drayton wanted to steal the slaves. Mr. Key, the prosecutor, had enlisted the help of another attorney, Richard Cox. Abby feared this older, more experienced man of the law might sway the jury to his side.

Abby entered the courtroom and took a seat in the back. The temperature in the courtroom was pleasant, a welcome change from last summer. Timothy Wood, the young reporter in her father's office, had already taken his seat in the front. He was tall, with dark hair, a broad forehead, a prominent nose, and a mustache. Her father said that even though he was young—eighteen years old— he was the most promising writer on the staff. She hoped he hadn't recognized her. It would be bad enough if word of her presence at the summer trial ever got back to her father, but if he were to learn she was missing school to be here, it would be even worse.

The jury trooped into the courtroom promptly at nine. Church bells, signaling the hour, heralded their entrance.

Abby watched the faces of the jury and was surprised not to see obvious traces of strain. Maybe she could rest easy this time. Had the jury found him not guilty? In Captain Drayton's previous trial, a few of the jurors had appeared so distraught that Abby wondered if they would make it through the day, let alone the week. But now no one appeared terribly shaken. The foreman rose to read the verdict. Abby, breathless, clung to the seat of her chair.

"The jury finds the defendant, Daniel Drayton, not guilty of stealing," he spoke firmly and decisively.

Abby could hardly believe her ears. *Justice has been served,* she thought. She wished she could share the news with Louisa.

Later, the prosecutors agreed to drop the remaining theft cases, but only if Captain Drayton accepted guilty verdicts for providing the means of transportation for the slaves. Mr. Mann, speaking for the captain, accepted the verdicts. The judge totaled the fines—$14,800. Mr. Mann had saved his client from life imprisonment, but in the end his victory proved bittersweet. Where would Daniel Drayton find $14,800?

After the trial ended, Abby's parents invited Mr. Mann and his supporters to their house. The fires were lit in both the parlor and the library. The Bailey children were told to wear their church clothes. Sara Jane Clarke, the children's governess, lent Abby a pale yellow dress made of tulle. The sleeves were puffed and the skirt long, full, and flowing. "You look radiant," her father said when she came downstairs.

Abby's mother, Margaret, loved to entertain and the Bailey home had become a gathering place for those committed to the anti-slavery movement. Their friends from Cincinnati and other parts of Ohio often stayed the night when they were in town. British abolitionists who raised money for the cause visited whenever they crossed the Atlantic. They came to the Baileys' house not only to discuss anti-slavery activities, but also to eat the delicious food Margaret and the cook Priscilla fixed—wild goose, veal rolls, mutton chops and buttered shrimps and turtle soup and beaten biscuits, sweet buns, and lemon cheesecakes, sweet potato pie, and spice cake.

Although the Baileys engaged in serious dinner conversation, afterwards they often amused themselves with games. Children of all ages as well as adults played charades—Margaret's favorite pastime. The younger people put on plays and anyone with a good voice was asked to sing.

On the evening of the verdict, Gamaliel discussed the judge's sentence with his guests. "It's a large amount to raise—a hefty sum, I'd say. That Philip is a shrewd character. He knew what he was doing when he insisted on seventy-four indictments for one so-called crime," he said, as he sipped his coffee in the parlor.

The men around him nodded in agreement. "And yet Captain Drayton was declared innocent of stealing. This is no small victory. I'd take a fine over twenty years in the penitentiary, wouldn't you, Dr. Bailey? As for the money— there are ways—there are always ways," said one of the guests.

Although Gamaliel himself never touched spirits, he would serve brandy to his guests. This loosened tongues and softened the hearts of any who indulged. John Candler, an abolitionist from London who was staying overnight at the Baileys, spoke out in his distinctly British accent, "When we return to London we shall tell our brethren of the capture of the *Pearl*, the plight of the slaves, and the sentencing. Rest assured our countrymen will not abandon the cause."

Mr. Candler had already traveled for a month, north to Boston and west to Ohio. Abigail's mother said he was ready to go home. He missed his wife and children who had stayed behind in London. The oldest was a daughter Abby's age and the youngest was just a baby. "The baby is going to be so big you won't recognize him," her mother had remarked before the other guests arrived. But before he could return Mr. Candler wanted to meet with a few more abolitionists in Philadelphia.

"All right now, ladies and gentlemen, it's time to teach our new guests blindman's bluff!" Abby's mother called out. Abby noticed that her mother looked especially pretty this evening. She was wearing a burgundy dress with stiff petticoats that gave the wide, full skirt a bell shape. The neckline bared part of her shoulders, but the long tight sleeves covered her arms. Her hair, a rich chestnut brown, was swept back and wrapped in a knot on top of her head, held in place with tortoise shell combs.

Margaret encouraged all her guests to play, often coaxing the most reluctant stragglers to join in the fun. "Come along, Abby, lend me a hand. Now, don't you think we should blindfold Mr. Mann?" she asked.

Before Mr. Mann had a chance to protest, Margaret was standing on her toes to tie a blindfold around his eyes. She made him turn around and gave him a little push. After just a few steps Mr. Mann bumped into a small end table. He turned and flailed his arms about like a man lost at sea. He touched a woman's sleeve and grasped the lace.

"Tell us, Mr. Mann, who do you think you've caught?" Margaret asked.

Mr. Mann appeared more flustered than Abby had ever seen him. Every day in court he had the look of someone so self-assured. Now he was totally beside himself.

"Why, Mr. Mann, I do believe you are squeezing my wrist!" the woman declared.

Mr. Mann recognized her voice and shouted out, "Mrs. Seaton, I beg your pardon." Mrs. Seaton, the mayor's wife, laughed as Mr. Mann removed his blindfold.

Margaret took the blindfold from Mr. Mann and called on another volunteer to take his place. When no one stepped forward, she declared it was Timothy Wood's turn to be blindfolded. Abby watched as his face turned beet red. *Why is Mother putting him through this?* she wondered. *This is not his usual practice. He'd rather have his nose in a book than play a parlor game.* Tim allowed himself to be blindfolded. He then proceeded to walk not in the general vicinity of the guests but in the opposite direction towards the library. Abby, hoping to discreetly inform him that he should reverse direction, tiptoed into the library. Just as she was about to let him know his error, he turned abruptly and, reaching out, hit upon her elbow. Abby held her breath as Tim tried to guess who she was. His hand brushed her hair and Abby thought she detected a slight tremble. His hand then gently touched her sleeve.

"Abigail Bailey—I presume," Tim announced with surprising certainty. He quickly removed his blindfold and smiled at Abby.

"You're right," Abby said, laughing.

Frances, Abigail's youngest sister, came running in and grabbed the blindfold from Tim. "It's my turn," she cried.

"All right. Let's see if you can catch someone before you go to sleep. Mother wants you in bed, but I suppose she won't mind if you take a short turn and don't get too excited," Abby told her sister.

"I'm going to catch everyone in the room," Frances said, jumping up and down.

"Oh no, you're not. Just one person and then off to bed. You know the rules and that's that. If you're not under the covers in fifteen minutes, it will be the end of you."

Frances paid no attention. "Here I come," she shouted, running off towards the parlor.

"I think you may have lost that battle," Tim said to Abby.

"Mother's always telling me to put her to bed, but Frances doesn't listen. You know how it is," Abby said.

"I suppose you have other things on your mind," Tim answered.

"What do you mean?" she asked.

"I mean besides taking care of your sister."

"I don't understand."

"I saw you today," Tim said.

Now it was Abby's turn to blush. "You didn't!" she gasped.

Tim nodded. "In the courtroom. You were in the back, weren't you?"

"Don't tell Father. You mustn't. I don't want to make him angry," she pleaded.

"My lips are sealed," he said pressing his finger to his mouth.

Abby felt he could be trusted, but at the same time wondered if he was laughing at her. Surely keeping her whereabouts from her father would not be one of his main priorities.

"You have a very special interest in that trial, don't you?" he asked.

"What makes you say that?" Abby answered.

"It's not the first time I saw you there," Tim explained.

"Here you are. I didn't see you in the parlor," Abby's father said, interrupting them as he entered the library.

Abby wasn't sure whether he was referring to her or to Timothy. She knew her father often enjoyed engaging Tim in long, political discussions. "The wisest eighteen year old I've ever come across," he liked to say. Timothy was also quite fond of her father, but surely he wouldn't tell her father she had attended the trial. She could not explain why but she felt her secret was safe with Tim.

Abby's father had told her that Tim had been expected to study law, but he showed little interest. He had only one goal—to work for an abolitionist newspaper. At the age of eighteen he sent letters to several editors and, when her father sent a positive response, Tim immediately took leave of his parents, left his home in Edenton, North Carolina, and moved to Washington.

"Mulled cider, anyone?" her mother asked as she passed a tray. Hot steam was rising from the china cups. It certainly was clear that no one was going to let them alone.

But later that evening, Timothy came up to Abby and asked in a soft voice, "Abby, will you walk me to the door?"

His boldness surprised her. At the door, he took his hat from the stand and said, "I was wondering if I could see you again. We could talk about the case, if you'd like."

Timothy turned and walked away before Abby had a moment to respond.

Chapter XIV
Roy

"We needs to move you where you can breathe more easy," Louisa said to Roy. Her stomach had stopped bothering her. If she summoned all her strength, she thought she could drag Roy out into the hall and then into the cargo room next door.

"I thought I'd be all right in here. Ain't no one gonna find me," Roy answered.

"I wouldn't be so sure," Louisa said. "I suspects someone's gonna find you, but you ain't gonna be among the living."

"I don't think I could stand on my own two feet," Roy cautioned.

"We'll see about that," Louisa said and then crossed behind him. She grabbed him under the arms and, stepping backwards, drew him towards her. Louisa heaved and pulled and eventually managed to drag Roy into the next room. The move was painful for Roy, but he appeared grateful nonetheless.

"You can stay hid behind these boxes. Ain't no one gonna come in here until we get to Liverpool," Louisa assured him.

Louisa gave Roy another sip of water and then sat down beside him. She needed to rest. "I went through this once before," she said. "I mean trying to escape and all, but things didn't turn out so good."

"This ain't my first time either," Roy answered. "But I'm wiser now. And you know something, I think I'm gonna to be lucky this time. I got a better sense of who's to trust and who ain't to trust. I once paid a white man $30 to help me get free. He took the money and said he'd find a way to get me to Ohio and after that everything would be easy. But he pocketed the money and then sold me to his friend."

Roy told Louisa he was born in a small town in Georgia called Madison. When he was only six years old, he was bought by a rice planter from South Carolina. He had never known his father and never saw his mother after he was sold. He was taken to Brightwood Plantation, a few miles from the coast, where he worked in the fields seven days a week. The skin on his bare back blistered under the hot sun. The overseer used his whip freely. Blood oozed down his back and dried, forming thick crusts on his blisters. Only at night could he find some relief, lying under huge live oaks, multiple threads of gray-green Spanish moss, like matted hair, dripping from their branches. At the age of seventeen he dared to run away, bringing with him the food he had collected, some smoked meat and bread. At the same time he decided to take the name 'Madison.' Never having been given a last name, he chose the name of his birthplace, the town he little remembered but a place that nevertheless felt a part of him.

Roy slept by day and walked by night, using the stars to guide him north. He ran out of food, hunted for corn and wild berries, was chased by dogs and caught in thunderstorms, and lost his way. Yet, miraculously, months later, he arrived in Philadelphia, many pounds thinner, his feet bruised and bloodied, his clothes torn, and a song in his heart.

He started to look for work, offering his services to the merchants, blacksmiths, and cabinet makers. He thought he was safe in Philadelphia, but he soon realized he was wrong. After two days spent seeking a job, he discovered that two men were following him. Everywhere he went, he could see them out of the corner of his eye, sometimes ducking behind a building, at other times turning to avoid coming face to face with him. He suspected they were slave catchers and did his best to elude them, but never succeeded. The men attempted to kidnap him, grabbing him at dusk on a deserted street. As they pinned him against a brick wall, he managed to escape their hold and fled in the direction of the wharf. The men ran after him, shouting "Thief!" An officer of the law, hearing their cries, questioned the men and then ran off in pursuit of Roy.

Roy heard the officer shout at him and panicked. He knew the kidnappers had called him a thief and assumed he stood no chance in a court of law. His word against the word of two white men—what chance did he have? He ran to save his neck. Arriving at the dock, he dashed up the gangplank, not stopping when the officer shouted his order, not thinking what course his future was taking. It was then that Louisa had gained her first glimpse of Roy.

Louisa listened to Roy's story and, when he was finished, again lifted the cup to his lips so he could take a sip of water. She and Roy both had been given second chances. If they could only manage to get to Liverpool without being arrested, they could taste real freedom for the first time.

Louisa slept fitfully that night. She worried that Roy might take a turn for the worse or that the wrong person might stumble in on him. She told herself she would check on him as soon as dawn broke. The hours passed slowly as Louisa waited for the first sign of daylight to come through the crack under the door.

The next morning Louisa slipped out of her cabin before breakfast and returned to the storage room. She found Roy still on the floor, but he was not the way she'd left him. He seemed a different person. His energy had been sapped. He was more listless than before, only

opening his eyes as she approached and then quickly
closing them. "I brought you some water and a little food,"
she whispered. She hadn't expected a moan in reply.
Louisa bent down and lifted Roy's head so he could sip
from the cup.

His sleeve was drenched in blood. "What happened
here?" she asked as she gently tried to lift his arm. But
the blood made the sleeve stick to the floor. The wound
must have opened up during the night and bled profusely.
"You'se got to get this clean," she said more to herself than
to Roy. He was not awake enough to respond. She put her
hand to his forehead and could feel the fever that was
taking over his body. Infection must have set in.

Stealthily Louisa crept out of the room. She returned
with wet compresses for bathing the wound. She wished
she could ask Bernice and Samuel for help, but she did
not dare. The idea of more people sneaking into the boiler
room worried her. Roy had taken her into his confidence—
she did not want to betray him. Besides, there were over
seventy passengers on this ship, many of whom she
thought she could trust, but still she was not sure about
everyone. If someone became suspicious, Roy's future was
doomed. It was best to keep his presence secret. *Just get
him to Liverpool,* she prayed. *Then he'll be safe.*

Louisa tore Roy's shirt so she could see the wound.
At the sight of his flesh her stomach muscles tightened.
She thought the most important step she could take would
be to clean the bloody area. She had never seen such a

deep wound and flesh so raw. She wiped away the dark stains from the skin. "You're gonna feel better soon," she whispered. After she finished with his arm, she put the remaining compress on his forehead. "That's to cool you down." Roy kept his eyes closed. *He sure can sleep soundly,* Louisa thought. She studied Roy's face, the brown skin glistening with sweat from the heated room and a feverish body, the distinctive eyebrows, his eyes closed, his eyelashes thick, his lips paler than his skin. Louisa liked being with him, but she did not want Bernice and Samuel to worry about her. "I'll check on you a little later," she whispered as she left. She knew he would not hear her, but she still spoke as if he were awake.

Over the next few days Louisa brought Roy water and food. Moist bread was all he could eat. She kept his wound clean and watched over him as his fever subsided. He slept less and talked more. She had no doubt his condition was improving. But on the fourth day she was not so sure. His skin became hot and moist. He barely opened his eyes. When he did his eyes looked unfocused. Roy had taken another turn for the worse—she could not deny that. He was worse than ever. She could no longer keep him in hiding. She hadn't wanted to tell anyone, but she would have to. *Of course I can trust Bernice and Samuel. Why am I worrying so?*

In trying to take care of him alone, she'd gotten in over her head. She couldn't raise him from the dead. If she was going to help him, she would have to act now.

Louisa mustered her courage and revealed her secret to Bernice and Samuel. When Louisa brought Samuel to the cargo room, Samuel took one glance at Roy and lost no time. He knelt beside Roy's body and took his pulse. "Go back to my cabin, Louisa. On the table you'll find a black case with some medicines in it. Quick. Go as fast as you can."

Telling Samuel had not been as bad as she feared. She wanted to explain that she never meant to cause any trouble. She'd heard the noise and discovered Roy and she couldn't just ignore him. She hadn't known what to do and she didn't want him to die. But then Samuel never made her explain anything. He didn't seem at all angry. Samuel asked her to stand watch over Roy to make sure he was going to be all right.

Louisa spent the night by Roy's side. When she caught herself drifting off to sleep a few times, she made herself stay awake by singing. She wasn't singing out loud, but she was singing in her head. Now that Samuel and Bernice knew about Roy, she didn't have to worry so much. It was an unexpected relief to know she wasn't the only one who shared Roy's secret. Trying to care for Roy on her own was more than she could handle.

Abby would be amazed if she knew what was happening. She'd really like Samuel and Bernice. They had told Louisa that once they got to England they'd meet British abolitionists who published articles in newspapers and organized speakers and helped the fugitives who had made it across the ocean. Bernice and Samuel planned to go around the country on a speaking tour to raise money to support abolitionist societies in the United States. Louisa couldn't wait to see this country. She'd heard she'd be able to eat with a white person in a tavern and sit next to one in church.

Of course Louisa was also hoping that by the time she got to Liverpool Roy would be well. And what's more, she didn't want him to get arrested before they got to Liverpool. She wasn't as worried for herself. Everyone on the boat thought she was free since she was traveling with Bernice and Samuel and could pass for their daughter. But now some of the passengers were whispering about "the stowaway with the deathly fever."

If only Roy hadn't gotten sick he might have been able to slip off the boat undetected. God was going to have to be on their side when they docked in Liverpool.

Chapter XV
Tim Wood

"You've done quite a fine job, Captain Drayton," Timothy complimented the captain on his penmanship.

Tim, the young *National Era* reporter, had taken to visiting Daniel Drayton in the jail where he had to stay a prisoner until the money could be raised to pay his huge fines. Tim had a knack for showing up when the captain was down and most in need of company. One day he brought a copy of the *National Era* with him. Daniel, who had never learned to read, asked to keep the newspaper. "I thought I'd just study these letters—now that I have the time, that is," he explained.

Tim answered, "You do that and the next time I come I'll see if I can't smuggle in a pen." With no light in his cell the only way Daniel could see was by sitting on the floor next to the grating. There he could catch a little light from the passageway. Although he could not read the words, he copied the headlines. It was a slow and tedious task. But soon, with Tim's help, he came to recognize the letters of the alphabet and to draw them more clearly.

Whenever Daniel heard the echo of the warden's footsteps on the cement floor, he quickly covered up the telltale evidence of his new occupation. But after the warden checked on him and the sound of footsteps faded, he again diligently pulled out his work and started again. The ABC's he drew at first appeared enormous and awkward, but over time his letters grew smaller. And Daniel had plenty of time.

"I thought I might try something different in a day or two. Suspect I might be graduating to Bible verses," Daniel told Tim.

Captain Drayton must be a quick learner, Abby thought. She had come with Tim to visit the captain. They had entered through the front door, walking through the guardroom where they obtained permission to visit the prisoner, past the office, kitchen, and sleeping quarters for the wardens, then up the steep, spiral staircase to the third-floor cell. The warden opened the heavy iron-grated door to Daniel's cell and then closed it behind them, locking it and pocketing the key. The floor was ice cold. Abby did not remove her cloak and neither of the men offered to take it.

Abby admired Tim for bringing in paper and pen. (It helped that Tim's frock coat was a hand-me-down from a rather large uncle which made it easier to conceal smuggled items.) Tim helped Daniel with his writing and he also became a friend, someone the captain could trust.

"I can't get over how much you've learned, Captain Drayton," Abby remarked.

The captain answered, "I always told myself I didn't want to die until I learned to read and write. And now it appears I'm to have my wish."

"Father says that the men in Boston are trying their best to help raise the money to free you and the other captain. Don't give up hope," Abby said.

"I'm a God-fearing man prepared to bide my time if need be, but I sure do hope the Lord will take notice," Daniel answered.

"I sneaked a little something for you out of the kitchen," Abby said, opening her satchel. "I suspect you'll rather enjoy it."

"You're keeping an eye out for me, ma'am and you know I am grateful," the captain said.

"Here you go," she said handing him the batch of lemon squares she had baked and wrapped in a linen towel.

"Why, I do thank you," the captain said, taking the package which warmed his hands. "It sure beats what they give us here." Tim had told Abby that the warden provided the captain with two meals a day, herring, cornbread, and a dish of molasses and water with a few drops of coffee for breakfast, more cornbread, salted beef, and soup made with cornmeal and a watery stock for dinner. Lemon squares had to be a welcome addition.

The sudden slamming of a door and the clanking of keys announced the return of the warden. Daniel quickly hid his paper, pen, and the lemon squares under his blanket. The cell was so sparsely furnished that it allowed no other hiding place. Any search could be accomplished in a matter of seconds.

"It seems to me you have been up to some mischief," the warden announced. Abby wondered what had aroused his suspicions. *Had he heard the paper rustling or smelled the freshly baked goods?*

"If I catch you up to something, I could take away your visitor privileges. You know that, don't you?" he added, turning to Tim. He seemed to enjoy the sound of his own loud, threatening voice.

Abby clenched her fists to stop her hands from trembling. She didn't want to make things worse by visiting. She thought her presence would cheer the captain up, not get him in trouble.

"I don't think you'll find fault with the prisoner, sir," Tim said.

The warden fixed his eyes on Tim and for a moment did not speak. Then he turned his head, looked at Abby, and spoke. "If it isn't Dr. Bailey's daughter! Why, you'd better let well enough alone and not go meddling in other people's business. Don't ask what happens when you get mixed up in things you shouldn't. Young ladies shouldn't set foot in a jail. Hard to say what might become of them.

Your father's a grown man and if he wants to be stirring up trouble, that's his affair. But you're too young for all that. You take my advice and you don't come near this jail again. You listen to me. Don't have anything to do with people who set out to break the law. You stay a mile away. That's what I tell my daughter. You don't catch her down here, now do you? When she leaves school, she goes home to study and I reckon that's where you should be now. Mark my words. You stay out of this jail or you're going to see and hear things you've never seen nor heard before."

Abby looked down at the cement floor. The warden was doing his best to scare her and he was pretty much succeeding. She didn't like what she heard, but if she talked back she would make things worse for the captain.

"What's the matter, young lady? Did you forget how to talk?" the warden shouted as he took her chin in his hand. Tim raised his arm as if to pull him away from her. The warden dropped his hand and said to Tim, "If you had the slightest bit of sense, you wouldn't bring her here. If I've said it once, I'll say it a thousand times—Young girls have no place here. Do you understand that?"

"I take it you're asking us to leave," Tim replied.

"I am indeed," the warden said. He held the door open for them.

Tim shook the captain's hand on his way out. Then, putting his arm on Abby's shoulder, he gently guided her down the long prison corridor in silence. They could hear the warden pacing behind them.

"He can't just make us leave like that, can he?" Abby asked, shaking with anger. "We have rights, you know. Has he done that to you before?"

"He doesn't like the idea of a girl visiting the jail," Tim answered.

They walked together away from the jail in silence until Tim said, "Your father tells me you knew the one slave who escaped from the jail."

"You mean Louisa," Abby said. Without thinking, she blurted out, "I'll tell you a secret I've never told anyone." There was something about the way Tim looked at her that made her think she could trust him. "You know how far she got that first night?" she asked.

"Into Maryland, I suppose," Tim answered.

"Not exactly," Abby said. "Not that night. She got as far as my house."

"You're not serious!" Tim replied.

"Yes. It's the absolute truth. And what's more—my parents, Marcellus, Frances, all my brothers and sisters—none of them knew. She slept in my room. I had to sneak food up to her. Our dog Charlie kept her company while I was at school."

"How long was she there?" Tim asked.

"A week. By the fourth day Louisa was about ready to scream. She just couldn't stand being cooped up. Louisa didn't want to spend her life in one room, just waiting, always wondering if her voice was going to be overheard or if her footsteps were too loud, never knowing if my parents would hear her or if she was going to get caught."

"Do you really think your father would get angry if he'd known she was there? He's given his life to end slavery."

"He has such strong feelings about the right way to do things," Abby answered. "He's never liked secrecy and he doesn't want to be put in a situation where he's forced to lie. He's always said he's a man of his word. He couldn't bring himself to lie if an officer questioned him. He just would not want to be part of something he had to keep secret."

"You made quite a gamble."

"My room's up on the top floor. I'm the only one up there."

"But still. It's just good you didn't get caught."

"I can hardly believe we tried to get away with it. Still at the time it seemed the only thing to do. I never wanted to upset Father. And I certainly didn't want to put the paper at risk. But Louisa was my friend."

Tim didn't answer. He wasn't going to challenge her.

Abby continued, "I think a lot about how his mind works, but I can't say I agree with him. There are just times when you decide that the laws are wrong and you're going to do whatever you can for the rights of the individual. And one of those basic rights is freedom. And if you have to lie to help someone become free, I say that's all right."

"I can't deny that. I'd have to take your side on this," Tim answered.

"I suppose you're wondering what happened to Louisa. Well, you've heard of Cousin Ruthie," Abby said. "It just so happened that she came to visit while Louisa was hiding in my room. It came out at dinner that night that Ruthie had helped a slave escape into Canada. So I got this idea that Cousin Ruthie could help Louisa too. I knew she couldn't stay in my room forever. She really hated living like a prisoner. That's how she felt confined to my room. Louisa was not afraid. So Louisa went off with Cousin Ruthie. Louisa's got to be the bravest person I know. They set off in a stagecoach. I kept thinking the next time I'd hear from Louisa she'd have made it to Canada—"

"You haven't heard yet?" Tim asked.

"Well, I did get a letter. But it wasn't from Louisa— it was from Cousin Ruthie. She said their stagecoach had been stopped in Delaware. One of the passengers warned Louisa that there was going to be a search. She'd have to produce papers. She panicked, opened the door, and escaped. She just ran off. Cousin Ruthie saw her disappear into the woods. And she's never been seen since."

Tim and Abby had arrived at the Baileys' house and they stood for a moment in front of the closed door. Before going inside, Abby said to Tim in a soft voice so no one could overhear, "You have to help me find her."

A few days later, at dusk, Abby stopped by her father's office to see Tim. She knew she had chosen a bad time as soon as she entered. Her father had his waistcoat unbuttoned. He was reading something—she was not sure what, but she could tell he was not pleased with it. Tim was writing feverishly and didn't even look up when she walked in the door. Abby thought she should turn around and come back later, but just as she started to go, Tim jumped up. "Abby," he shouted. "Don't leave yet."

"You looked so busy. I didn't want to bother you."

"I've got to get this story done. But I do have some great news. About Louisa. I think she fell into good hands," Tim whispered.

"What?" Abby asked.

"Meet me outside in an hour," Tim called out to Abby.

Abby waited on the street a little more than an hour. She heard the bell chime once, signaling the half hour. The sky had grown dark, but it was only half past five. The days were all too short. The only good thing about that was that it meant Christmas was coming. She didn't want to go back inside because she knew her father would only think she was keeping Tim from his work. Tim would look for her as soon as he got a chance.

"Abby, there you are," Tim said rushing out the door which made a loud noise as it swung shut. He grabbed her arm and started pulling her down the street. "I thought I'd never finish."

"Quick. Tell me about Louisa," Abby pleaded.

"Last night I was talking to my friend, Benjamin Sturge. You know the one who lives across the river in Alexandria. He's a Quaker and he's always traveling back and forth to Philadelphia. He started telling me this story and before long I realized he must be talking about Louisa—"

"Are you sure?" Abigail asked. "Is she all right?"

"Yes, that is, I think so. That is, she was doing fine the last he heard," Tim answered. "When she ran off from your Cousin Ruthie, she escaped into the woods in Delaware, not far from Philadelphia. She might have starved, but a young boy found her and brought her back to his house. It was a Quaker family. They took her in and fed her. Benjamin was visiting and he remembers meeting her."

"I can hardly believe it. You're sure it's the same Louisa?"

"I guess we can't be absolutely sure. I know he said the girl's name was Louisa and he thought she looked fifteen, give or take a year. He couldn't say one way or the other about who was with her before she ran off into the woods. So I can't say she was with your Cousin Ruthie, but I do know she escaped from a stagecoach. Abby, it's just got to be the same Louisa."

"If it is the same Louisa, then she's just outside Philadelphia!" Abby said breathlessly.

"Well no, not exactly," Tim answered. "When Benjamin returned a month or so later she was gone."

"Did he find out where she went?"

"He didn't ask. Abby, people don't ask many questions about fugitives," Tim said. "It's better not to know."

"But I just want to know if she's safe."

"Abby, I have a feeling she must be in good hands," Tim assured her. "That family must have looked out for her."

"Tim, we have to go see Louisa's parents. Maybe they've heard something. And if they haven't, then at least we can give them this news."

"Do you mean now?" Tim answered.

"Yes."

Abigail smiled and led Tim towards Georgetown. They walked at a brisk pace. Abby pulled her coat tightly around her neck and Tim put his arm around her shoulder. They came to a field of tall grass; on the other side lay Georgetown. The wind had picked up and was blowing so hard that it pushed them across the clearing. They reached the cobblestone road and then made a sharp right.

The street was dimly lit by a gas lamp. Abby and Tim circled the senator's house, finding their way to the slave quarters in the back. They would not be the only guests this evening. A huge group of people stood outside. The door was open and the crowd was slowly making its way inside. Everyone was wearing Sunday-best clothes.

Many of them carried huge baskets of food. A sudden lump in Abby's throat made it hard for her to swallow. She was not sure if she wanted to go on. Tim took her hand. They both knew that people only gathered together like this for two reasons—a wedding or a funeral.

Chapter XVI
London

At dusk Louisa left the house to walk through the city. The streets always collected dirt and heavy dust hung in the air. When she wiped her brow, her clean crisp handkerchief turned black. But she didn't care about the dirt so much. She enjoyed feeding the pigeons, sitting under a tree in Hyde Park, or walking along the banks of the River Thames. What she liked best was seeing the people on the street—she recognized many of them and some even smiled at her. She didn't have to carry a pass when she left the house. No one ever asked her for one or made her feel she didn't belong. Only a few stared at her. Maybe they had not seen many black people so they were just curious. It wasn't that they didn't like the way she looked. The pie man always nodded to her. The orange girl got to know her, as did the other hawkers selling fruits and vegetables.

Something about London made her feel at home. The city was different from Liverpool where the ship had docked. Liverpool was dark and gloomy and foreboding.

There she'd been so worried about Roy that she didn't fully realize she was finally setting foot in a free country. Everyone had been rushing to get on shore. People were pushing and bumping into one another. Samuel was leading Roy off the boat. Since Roy was putting most of his weight on Samuel, Bernice and Louisa carried all the luggage. Once on shore, they rushed to find a doctor. Roy's fever was so high that she wasn't sure they'd be able to get him to one in time. But they did manage to get him to a doctor who told them he was going to be all right. Roy needed to stay under the doctor's care for a few weeks and then he would be able to travel.

As Roy and Louisa parted she urged him to take care of himself. He pressed his hand in hers and whispered, "Thank you. You saved my life." He promised to come to London as soon as he recovered fully. "I'd like to see you again," he explained. "That is, if you'd like to see me," he added, stuttering over the words.

It wasn't until Samuel, Bernice, and Louisa got everything loaded into the stagecoach and headed for London that it began to hit Louisa that now she was indeed free. No one was going to come after her again. No one was going to arrest her, or threaten her, or beat her, or tell her how to live her life. She looked up at Bernice and Samuel sitting across from her. They were resting their heads against the back of the seat—their eyes closed. Tears filled Louisa's eyes as she studied their sleeping faces.

How could these people, perfect strangers only a few weeks ago, have been so good to her? Of all the young slaves in Washington, of all the slaves all over the South, why had she been chosen? Why was she the one riding in this stagecoach?

Six weeks later, once settled in London, Louisa was back to doing laundry again. That wasn't what she thought she would do. Still, it wasn't all that bad. She didn't have to just do laundry all day. She got to do other things as well. Bernice and Samuel had asked their friend, a British abolitionist, to help find her a job. Now here she was working as a regular housemaid for a family in London. She had to get up before dawn and help light all the fires. Then, she would bring fresh water to all the rooms so the master and the mistress, their children, and guests could bathe. Lady Baxter liked to keep to a schedule and have everything in order. She expected the servants to accomplish their routine chores efficiently and promptly.

The house was always made to appear tidy with each knickknack in its place. The china closet was a sight to behold. Louisa could gaze for hours at the stacks of plates. She grew quite fond of the pretty willow pattern in a dark shade of green. Other cabinets were lined with glistening crystal, carefully towel-dried so no fingerprints would show.

The housekeeper was good to Louisa and did not yell, not even when Louisa spilled the bath water on the stairs.

Instead of getting angry, the housekeeper said, "Look, your arm's all red—you've scalded it." And she made her put cold water on it. Louisa didn't have to worry about getting whipped. She knew that just wasn't going to happen. *Not that it's perfect,* she thought. *But it's a far cry from what I was used to.*

If she did a poor job, she might find herself without work, but that was the worst that could happen. No one would treat her the way they did in America or leave her with welts on her back, the way they left her mother. Ironing the linens wasn't as bad as it once had been. Keeping everything starched and unwrinkled wasn't an easy job, but on cool days the steam felt good on her face.

Louisa shared a room in the house on Park Lane with three other scullery maids. The four of them each laid claim to a corner of the room, a bed and a small table. They kept their belongings in chests under the beds. Louisa didn't have much of anything when she arrived, but she'd started to acquire a few things, most of them handed down to her by the lady of the house, Cecilia Baxter. The other maids' skin was white. They didn't seem to notice that hers was different—at least they never talked about it. They didn't ask about America or her past. They were perfectly content to discuss only the present and to ignore the world she had left behind. She thought they did not wish to pry. They made her feel welcome, and yet there remained a certain distance.

What she liked best about her new life was feeling the coins in her pocket on the days she got paid. She enjoyed rubbing the coins together and listening to the sound they made. She was stunned when the housekeeper handed her two shillings. This was the first time she'd ever kept the pay for her work. On her first afternoon off, she ran all the way to the boardinghouse where Bernice and Samuel lived. She burst in the door and took the silver coins out of her pocket to show them. Then, she found a cloth and polished them until they shone. Later that evening, back on Park Lane, she placed them on the table next to her bed. They were the last thing she saw at night before she blew out the candle and the first thing she saw in the morning. The money reminded her that she was no longer a slave—she earned her own wages.

Bernice told her she wouldn't be a housemaid forever. She and Samuel were giving lectures now to support the anti-slavery cause. They told her they had a grand plan which she could be a part of if she chose. They were going to open a dry goods store. As soon as they found a location and made the necessary arrangements, she could work as a clerk. She'd like arranging the merchandise and talking to the customers. In the meantime, she would keep working for Lady Baxter.

Bernice and Samuel were as good to her as they would be to their own child. But sometimes Louisa didn't enjoy being around them because it only made her miss her own parents more. She wanted to let her parents know that this time her escape had not failed. Not only that but she had made it all the way across the ocean. Abby would get word to them that she was safe once Abby got her letter. But there was no way of knowing how long that would take. And until then her parents would know nothing. They'd have to trust in the Lord.

She hoped her father's leg was better. She hated thinking of him in pain. It was hard not knowing how he was doing. Everything about her life had changed now. And it was all so sudden. She couldn't talk to her mother anymore. She couldn't see her baby brother grow up. *It's best if I just don't let myself think about them,* she thought. But of course that was impossible. She could see them in her mind's eye as clearly as they appeared the day she left.

Once in a while Louisa would ask herself if she'd lost her mind. *I just walked away from what was once my life,* she thought. Although she really hated some things about it, there were parts of her life she hadn't wanted to give up. Hadn't Abby's Cousin Ruthie warned her leaving was going to be hard? "Worth it, but still hard," she'd said. Ruthie had wanted her to realize what she was getting into. "You know you won't be able to turn back." Those were her words. Of course she'd known that, but she hadn't realized how many little things she'd miss. Like the ripples on the Potomac River when she and Abby would throw rocks across the water. Or burning her tongue on the cinnamon coach wheels which she liked to taste as soon as Abby's mother pulled them out of the oven. Or Sunday mornings, when she'd stand in church and look around her at all the people singing praises to the Lord. The sound was loud and joyful and deafening. She hadn't heard anything like it since she crossed the ocean.

She wondered if she'd ever see Abby again. She supposed she'd have to wait for Abby to make a trip to London. If Abby's father came to England to raise money for the newspaper, he might bring Abby along. Of course she didn't know how quickly that would happen. She couldn't let herself count on it anytime soon. But, whenever she saw Abby, things would be the way they'd always been. She'd like to introduce her to Bernice and Samuel. She'd already told them so much about Abby that sometimes she forgot they'd never even met her.

The days were getting shorter as Christmas approached. All of London was taking on a festive appearance. Lady Baxter requested decorations everywhere and she kept the servants hard at work—cleaning, polishing, and arranging the greens. Louisa heard the other servants talk about parties and overnight guests and presents— something about Boxing Day and boxes filled with money.

Martin, one of the servants in the kitchen, had taken a liking to Louisa from the first day he saw her. Sometimes she'd be hard at work and she'd look up and discover

Martin not working, but just staring at her. She found the attention flattering and she rather enjoyed talking to him. He was the only one who ever asked her about America. He said he'd always hoped to go there because he stood a good chance of finding better work. Many of his Irish kin were taking boats to go there. Talking with Martin made Louisa wonder. It just didn't make sense. Here she'd risked her life to get to England while Martin's family was sailing to America.

Louisa enjoyed Martin's company, but the boy who had captured her heart was Roy. They'd gotten to be such good friends on the boat as she helped him regain his health. *Surely he'll recover and find a way to come to London just as he promised*, she thought. They were both strangers in a foreign land. Their families remained on the other side of the ocean. But it was more than this that had brought them together. There was something about Roy. He knew what she was thinking before she opened her mouth. She could shut her eyes and remember him in the steam room, his head on her lap, his eyes looking into hers. She knew then that he cared for her. He would leave Liverpool as soon as he was able.

All the servants spent extra time in the kitchen to prepare for the Christmas holiday. Louisa had never seen a kitchen so well equipped. Wonderful smells filled the house for days on end. The cook put Louisa in charge of chopping the apples for the mince pies—it took an entire afternoon to empty the barrel of apples. Together the servants mixed them with nuts, shredded brisket, suet, brandy, and spices—nutmeg, cinnamon, and cloves. There was talk of preparing a boar's head for the Christmas Day dinner and it was said that the servants ate as well as their master and mistress.

When Louisa went out after dark, she took special pleasure in the doors festooned with wreaths and the iron lampposts wrapped with garlands. She would look into the neighbors' windows and catch a glimpse of the fir trees lit with candles. Sometimes she crept up to the window and peered inside, gazing at the tree ornaments which sparkled with reflected candlelight. Her mother would like seeing how pretty all the houses looked. *Mama thought I was doing the right thing,* Louisa reminded herself. *She wasn't scared. She knew the Lord was goin' to look after me.*

Louisa was carrying a basket of linens when her Christmas wish came true. It was the day the coal was delivered—only a week before Christmas. As she came through the door and stepped into the hall she realized she was not alone. On the other side of the room stood a young man with a coal scuttle in one arm and a heavy load under the other. Although he was turned away from her, she recognized him immediately. The shape of his back, the way he held his shoulders, even the slight tilt of his head were familiar to her. She called his name and he turned to face her. Dropping his load of coal, he came towards her. Louisa felt the blood rise to her face and heard her heart beating. She looked at Roy transfixed and could not utter a word. If a ghost had appeared before her, she could not have been more surprised.

Then Roy started talking and his words came tumbling out. He said he was so glad to see her. He'd missed her—words she had been dreaming he would say. Roy talked quickly as if he thought their time together would be taken away from them.

Roy had gained his strength back in Liverpool. He told Louisa he'd gotten a job hauling wood and saved enough money to get to London. He wanted to see Louisa the moment he set foot in the city, but he persuaded himself he needed to find work first. He wanted to surprise her with his health restored, a roof over his head, and a job with wages that were his to keep and not hand over to a master. He'd gone to the wharf where he found other men looking for jobs. "Go talk to Mr. Jennings," they said and pointed to an older man with small eyes, thin lips, and rough skin. Mr. Jennings coughed and sputtered and spat and finally consented to offer Roy a job as a coalporter.

Roy took the job. He rose early and spent every hour of daylight unloading coal from the ships on the Thames and then transporting it to people's homes. On his first free morning he tracked down Bernice and Samuel. That wasn't hard. On one of his coal delivery stops he'd overheard a

conversation and realized he was in the home of a Mr.
Dickerson, a British abolitionist. He inquired about Bernice
and Samuel—no strangers to Mr. Dickerson's abolitionist
circle. Roy received directions to their boardinghouse.
Bernice and Samuel were delighted to see Roy in good health
and gave him Lady Baxter's address. Roy then arranged
with Mr. Jennings to deliver coal to Lady Baxter.

And now, here he was. "I knew I would find you. I
mean—I was hoping you might still want to see me and
then—" Roy didn't finish his sentence. Louisa saw the soot
from the coal that had rubbed onto his cheeks and brow
and then she looked into his eyes and she knew that he
did still care for her. He had never stopped caring for her.
She'd been on his mind the whole time. All these weeks
when she was wondering what had become of him, he was
thinking about her.

"Want to see you!" Louisa was practically shouting.
Then she added in a softer voice, "Of course I want to see
you."

They talked for a few more minutes and then Roy
said he had to make his next delivery. But he would meet
her that night after work. He would be on the street
waiting for her.

Louisa retrieved the basket of linens she had dropped
and, still breathless, climbed the stairs. "He said he was
going to meet me. He said he would wait for me," Louisa
said, talking to herself. When she got to the top, she looked

up to see the housekeeper waiting for her. Louisa thought for a moment that the housekeeper would be angry with her for talking to Roy, but the housekeeper had a smile on her face. "Who was that you were talking to?" she asked and, without waiting for an answer, added, "I think he likes you."

Chapter XVII
The Letter

"I have a letter for Abigail Bailey." The deep voice resounded through the house.

"I can give it to her if you'd like," Abby's brother Marcellus answered.

"No, I must give it to her directly," the young man declared.

"If you insist." Marcellus turned to the stairs and called out to his sister, "Abby, you have a caller!"

As she descended the stairs, Abby caught her first glimpse of her visitor. "Tim, it's you!" She sounded happy to see him. They had not seen each other since the night they had visited Louisa's family. Tim looked into Abby's eyes and smiled. "I have something that will bring you great pleasure," he said, handing her a letter.

Abby took the letter and held it with two hands as she examined the handwriting.

"Oh, Tim! I can hardly believe it!" Abby's trembling fingers broke the seal as she spoke. "Tim, how did you ever get this? How can I ever thank you!"

"My friend Ben. It seems he's been back in touch with his friends in Delaware," Tim answered smiling.

London, October 21, 1848

Dear Abby,

Yes, I'm writing you from London! You see the journey didn't go exactly as planned. I never made it to St. Catharine's and I never got to see Niagara Falls. But I did make it to a free country and I can hardly believe my good fortune. Now I don't have to worry about who sees me or who hears me. I'm not always looking over my shoulder. I can walks down the streets and I can go in shops and no one gonna treat me like I don't belong. Here we don't have to hide the fact that we can read and write. People I meet, they act like I'm a real person. Some of them even asks me questions. They think I have a story to tell and they want to listen.

Once in a while I believe this place comes pretty close to paradise, but then I remembers my mother and father and the baby. This is a place they ain't never gonna see. I starts wondering if I'll ever get to see them again. Sometimes when I close my eyes all I can see is my father with his leg all swollen. He was in a lot of pain when I left. Mama was worried sick. He kept her up nights with his moaning. I miss them, Abby. But that don't mean I regret my decision. Mama would have gone and done the same thing given the chance. She wanted me to have my freedom. She don't want me to spend the rest of my life working for Missus Frye, doing nothing but scrubbing and ironing and not allowed to go where I pleases.

Of course I do have a few precious memories like wading in the river and the games we use to play on the island. The food here ain't the same. Nobody makes spice cake or coach wheels like your mother's.

One day, Abby, I will tell you what happened after I left Washington in the company of your Cousin Ruthie. There were some good people I met along the way. But there's one special person I do have to tell you about. His name is Roy and I think he likes me. I met him on the boat coming over. He was hiding and I done found him. I didn't tell no one until I had to. I had to because he was very sick. But he made it thru. We were two of the lucky ones. When I sees him on the boat, I thinks he is gonna die. Now that I left Liverpool, I don't know when I'll ever see him again. I knows he plans to come to London and I always keeping my eye out for him.

I work as a servant now, but I should be helping out in a shop soon—a dry goods store, to be exact. The housekeeper where I am now is real nice to me. She always wants to make sure I get enough to eat. And when I was new at the job she was very good about explaining things. She's not one of these people who make you think you should know everything before you even start work.

The candle on my table is now quite short. I must blow it out. I need to rise tomorrow with the first sign of light and fill all the basins with water before my master and mistress awake. I would have writ sooner, but it was hard to find the right person to deliver my letter. I finally found someone I can trust. He's sailing to Philadelphia on Thursday. It may take more than a fortnight, but one way or another this letter is bound to reach you. I've learned that fugitives have friends we do not know in strange places. Please try to get word to Mama and Papa that I arrived safely. Life is sweet to me, but I miss all of you and I even miss Washington and the banks of the Potomac.

Yours truly,

Louisa

A tear slid down Abby's cheek as she finished the letter. Part of her felt so happy for Louisa. She had a better life now and new friends and all these dreams that were starting to come true. Another part of her felt sad. The problem was there was something Abby needed to tell Louisa.

Abby had known for two weeks, but there was no way to get in touch with Louisa. Now she would have to let Louisa know, and yet she hated to be the one to spoil her happiness. *I can't put if off. Not even for a day,* she thought. She would ask Tim to give her letter to his friend Ben. Surely Ben would have a way of getting a reply back to Louisa.

Chapter XVIII
Christmas Eve

On Christmas Eve, the housekeeper pulled Louisa aside after she had finished her work. Her skin, full of wrinkles, was still soft and rosy colored. "You're going out now, are you?" she remarked, not really expecting an answer. "I have something for you. I was going to wait until Boxing Day, but I just couldn't. Here, take it. You can open it now. Go on, let me see if you like it."

The housekeeper handed Louisa a box tied shut with a perfect bow. She took the gift and slid off the silk ribbon. She removed the top, looked inside, and gasped, pulling out a delicate silver chain with a heart-shaped locket. "This is for me?" she asked incredulously. How could all this good fortune come to her? She held the gleaming silver up to the light and smiled.

"You'll need to polish it now and then," the housekeeper explained.

"Thank you so much. This is the nicest present anyone ever gave me! I'll wear it around my neck and never take it off." Louisa gave the housekeeper a hug and kissed her cheek. "Merry Christmas," she added.

"Now, you run along and have a nice evening. But remember your work day starts early tomorrow. Lady Baxter expects a big breakfast and a warm fire in the morning."

Louisa turned to go. Roy would be expecting her and she wanted to show him her new locket.

"But wait, I can't believe I almost forgot. There's something else. Here, this was delivered this afternoon—for you," the housekeeper said as she handed Louisa a letter. "In time for Christmas," she added, smiling.

Louisa could hardly believe what was happening. It was too good to be true. She had never, ever, worn, let alone owned, a locket or a brooch. The present, her first piece of jewelry, and now this, her first letter. News from home. She ran outside, her fingers clutching the letter and crushing the envelope in her excitement.

A gentle snow was falling on the city streets, covering traces of soot and grime. The air felt clean and crisp. The snow glistened as it reflected the light from the gas lamps. Roy was waiting for her. As he stood bareheaded on the stoop, the snow dusted his hair. Roy grabbed her hand and the two gazed into the night. A carriage, pulled by a handsome stallion, whisked by. The sound of the horse's hooves echoed in the distance. With every passing minute the night was more magical. Here they were in London, the most beautiful city she'd ever even imagined. In the distance she could see cathedral spires. As she listened to the church bells ring, she thought that they marked the growing number of days she spent as a free person. Just a few short months ago, neither she nor Roy had been sure they would make it to this country both alive and well. But they each had made it. Everything that happened—it was all more than she had wished for.

"Look, it's my first letter," she told Roy as she broke the seal on the letter. "It's from Abby! I knew she'd write back as soon as she figured out where I was."

Almost quivering, Louisa started to read the letter. By the time she reached the end, her eyes welled with tears, smearing the blue ink and blurring the words on the page.

Washington, November 30

Dear Louisa,

I was so excited to receive your letter. You have no idea what a case of nerves I've had. Charlie knew something was wrong. He followed me around and looked up at me with his sorrowful eyes as if he wanted to be petted when what he actually wanted was to comfort me. But then I got your letter and now I'm reassured. I kept hearing horrible stories of the fugitives who were captured on the *Pearl*. They were sold to the worst kind of masters. Emily, the girl you met on the boat, has had a terrible time. You remember her mistress would not take her back so she was put on a ship and sent down to New Orleans to be sold along with her sister Mary. Then once they took them down there, yellow fever swept through New Orleans. The dealer ended up bringing all the slaves back and is keeping them in a slave pen in Alexandria. It is just like being locked up in jail. Emily's parents want to buy their daughters' freedom. But they are going to have to raise a lot of money—$2,250!

Every once in a while, you hear about someone making an escape. I was praying you would be one of the lucky ones. And now I learn you have gone all the way to London. I could hardly believe you were writing me from the other side of the ocean! I have always wanted to go there. Maybe I could convince Mother and Father to let me visit you. You will have to show me around. Those people who visit my father always talk about St. Paul's Cathedral. They make it sound so grand.

Tim Wood, the reporter who works for Father at the *National Era*, brought me your letter. He has friends who are Quakers and one of them got hold of it and delivered it to Tim. Your letter really lifted my spirits. I had been worried sick about your whereabouts. You know who has been asking about you? Cousin Ruthie! She keeps writing to see if I have heard from you. Since I hadn't heard I did not write back and that just set her to worrying even more. She wrote that the water cure at Glenhaven went well. She found the setting quite beautiful and the water colder than she would have liked, but "undoubtedly beneficial" (her words). She thinks highly of Dr. Gleason and is trying to get Father to take the cure.

I wanted so much to attend Captain Drayton's trial. Of course I could not tell my parents because I knew how disturbed they would be, especially my father. (He has not stopped thinking I am too young to hear about what goes on in the world.) During the summer I was always trying to slip out of the house without telling Mother where I was going. I was so scared someone would see me and tell my parents. The courthouse was always very crowded and I guess no one paid any attention. In any case word never got back to my parents.

Horace Mann, the congressman from Massachusetts, took on the defense. The verdict came back "guilty" the first time the case was tried. They found him guilty of STEALING slaves.

But then there was an appeal and Mr. Mann tried really hard to get him freed. I guess you would say we won and we also lost. The prosecution (that was handled by the district attorney, Philip Barton Key) was accusing Captain Drayton of two crimes—stealing the slaves and helping to transport them. Mr. Mann managed to prove Captain Drayton was not trying to steal them, but he had to plead guilty to the transportation charges. So now he and Captain Sayres have to stay in jail until they can pay their fines. (As you can imagine this amounts to a rather large sum, especially since they were fined separately for each of the fugitives on the boat. The total sum comes to $14,800 for Captain Drayton and $11,100 for Captain Sayres.)

Tim Wood attended the trial and wrote about it for the paper. Father says he is the best reporter on the staff. I am starting to get to know Tim—he's a very nice person. He visits Captain Drayton in jail and is helping him learn to read. I've been with him a couple times. The jail is such a dreadful place.

I have waited until the very end to pass on something that is painful and sad. I know I cannot keep it a secret. I have saved it for last because I am not at all sure how to write it. It concerns your father. You told me he had been sick and that your mother had to work days and nurse him all evening, but I did not know how sick. I didn't know he was not going to survive. Your father's life ended two weeks ago. There, now I said it. Louisa, I am so sorry. I just wish it did not have to be true. I do not know what to add except that your father will not have to suffer anymore in this world. He is at peace now.

I found out sort of by accident. I told Tim about you. Then the two of us went by the senator's to see your parents. But, when we arrived, we saw a huge crowd of people. It was very distressing. They were all preparing for the funeral. I had not heard that he had died and I was just walking into the middle of it. I knew you did not know of course and I could not imagine where you were and I kept thinking how strange it was that this was all going on and you did not have any idea what was happening. But now I have told you. And I just hope you will take some comfort in knowing there were so many people who were bringing food and wanting to take care of your mother. But of course your mother was the one making everyone else feel better and telling them that they were all going to meet up again in the next world. "Our life on earth is so short," she'd say, "but God's resting place is everlasting."

Your friend,

Abby

Chapter XIX
Freedom Calls

Tim spent many winter evenings at the Baileys. He often arrived unannounced, under the pretense of asking Dr. Bailey a question concerning the newspaper. Sometimes he showed him a draft of a story and asked for his advice, or he would seek his opinion on a certain issue, such as a debate in Congress or a set of resolutions proposed by a group of abolitionists. Tim always came armed with a subject for discussion, but ever hopeful that he would catch a glimpse of Abby and perhaps enjoy her company as well.

On several occasions Abby's mother asked Tim to stay for dinner. Afterwards Dr. Bailey would step outside to smoke his pipe, leaving Abigail and Tim inside. Abby often asked Tim if he might not be hiding another letter from Louisa in his pocket. But it was March before Tim produced such a letter.

"I knew if I waited long enough I'd finally hear from her," Abby shouted. She was so excited that she grabbed the letter and threw her arms around Tim. Then, flustered

that she had acted so impulsively, she started to laugh and
pulled her arms back.

Abigail sat down in her father's chair in the library
and brushed a lock of hair out of her face. She checked the
date on the letter and saw that it had taken more than
two months to reach her. She read the letter first silently,
and then out loud to Tim.

London, January 18, 1849

Dear Abby,

Your letter arrived on Christmas Eve. You always
think good things are suppose to happen on Christmas,
not bad things. I knew how sick Pa was and that when I
left Washington I might never see him again. Not that
I came out and actually admitted it. Was that the price
I had to pay for the freedom I won? I try not to think
that my leaving troubled him and that worrying made
him sicker. I ain't gonna allow myself to think like that.
If there's one thing I am learning it's that you can't
keep looking back. God put us on this earth to move
forward. Mama knows he is in heaven and she will join
him there when her time comes. When I finished your
letter, I wanted so much to run to Mama and have her
catch me in her arms. But I knows that could not be so,
seeing as how we had an ocean between us. And seeing
as how I would be whipped and sent away and sold to
Lord knows who if I ever show my face again, I cannot
turn around now. When I stepped onto the stagecoach

with your Cousin Ruthie, I says to myself I ain't gonna set foot in Washington again.

There's someone who helped me through all this. I don't think I could do it alone. His name is Roy. He is a true friend and always was ever since I done met him on the boat. I told you about him in my first letter. He just seems to know what I'm feeling and he wants me to know that he cares about me.

One day, the best day, he just showed up at the house where I work. He'd taken a job as a coalporter. He seemed quite happy to see me. Roy says he does not want to be a coalporter forever. He received a gunshot wound when he was trying to escape and that's why I thought he was gonna die. After he got off the boat he went to a doctor for treatment and he decided then and there that he wanted to be an apprentice to a surgeon. But until he can find someone willing to take him on, he's gonna deliver coal.

Of course I can't close without asking about Christmas. I'm sure that your holiday was full of good cheer. And I'm sure you ate lots of delicious food and that your parents had a party with music and games. You probably played charades too. I remember the times you and me spent in the kitchen during those parties. We could always hear the laughter and the loud talking through the closed doors.

Please try to visit Mama as soon as you are able. Tell her I love her and I miss her. Ask her to put a

flower on Pa's grave for me. Give my baby brother a
kiss for me. And please let my mother know I am safe
and in good hands. She mustn't worry about me.

Yours truly,

Louisa

The following evening, after dinner, Abby went to her
room, lit the oil lamp, and gathered paper and pen. Sitting
down at her writing table, she began a letter to Louisa. It
was past midnight before she finished.

By the time Abigail's letter reached Louisa, spring
had come to London. With the new season London was
transformed. For a month it had rained everyday and now
suddenly the sun was shining. Roy and Louisa went for
long walks along the banks of the Thames and talked about
their future. A warm spring breeze gently shook the
budding trees. The grass was a rich green and daffodils
were everywhere in bloom. The pigeons reappeared, taking
over their old haunts on rooftops and street corners.

Sometimes Louisa would surprise Lady Baxter by
returning home with armfuls of flowers that she and Roy
had picked—pink roses, violet larkspur, yellow forsythia.
Once she walked in the house with bunches of blooming
lilacs. Their strong scent filled the air. The housekeeper,
overjoyed, helped her arrange them in vases and put them
throughout the house. Lady Baxter was pleased and
thanked her for providing such a bountiful harbinger of
spring, "and so very fragrant."

"Come closer, Louisa," Lady Baxter said as she beckoned her to her side. She wore an elegant pale blue dress, with a white lace collar. Taking hold of Louisa's wrist, she said, "You bring good cheer wherever you are. With that, you will go far wherever it may be."

Not long afterwards, sometime in early May, the housekeeper handed Louisa a letter addressed with her name. Louisa, still in her apron, ran outside, ripping open the letter. She read the letter once quickly, and then again slowly.

Washington, March 24, 1849

Dear Louisa,

Your letter arrived yesterday! I wanted to let your mother know I had heard from you so Tim and I visited her this afternoon. We found her outdoors, taking care of her bees. I gave her your messages and read parts of your letter out loud to her. Then the three of us went to the Mount Zion burying grounds. Your mother brought your little baby brother. (He seems very healthy and has quite a bit of fat on him.) The wind blew fiercely that afternoon and it did not feel much like Easter. Tiny white petals ripped from the trees swept through the air, falling to the ground, dusting the gravestones. Your mother carried a bouquet of Easter flowers from the senator's house. We put the flowers on the grave the way you wanted. There is a gray stone marker on your father's grave.

Your mother was singing. I can still hear her. "I looked over Jordan and what did I see. A band of angels lookin' after me. Comin' for to carry me home." It's a peaceful place. Your mother says whenever she goes there she feels your father's presence. "Sometimes I feel he is right there next to me and he can hear every word I say." She believes your father knows you made the right choice and that he must be singing praises to the Lord that you are free.

This evening Father wanted to have a serious conversation with me. He began discussing the newspaper and what it meant to be an abolitionist. He said you always should stand up for what you believe in. And that things don't always have to stay the way they are. "There comes a time when you must demand change." I wasn't expecting this at all. You know how he's always thinking I'm not old enough to understand certain things. It's odd because in his work he tries hard to expose evil and do away with it, but when he gets home all he can think about is protecting us "little ones." He forgets we're not so little anymore.

But tonight was different. I started talking to him about you and your family. I told him how your mother had been born free, but sold into slavery. I said you were determined not to spend the rest of your life in slavery. Then I explained that you had escaped to London. I left out the part about your hiding in my room.

He looked at me and let his glasses slip down on his nose. I could tell he was surprised and really happy that you were safe. He did not ask any questions. He just listened to what I had to say. Then he said he thought people needed to hear your story. "If we can just get people to face the truth, they will put an end to slavery," he said.

As far as I can tell he still does not suspect you were hiding here or that you left Washington with Cousin Ruthie! I know some day I will have to tell Mother and Father, but it can wait.

You were wise to leave the country. There is just no telling what would happen to you if you stayed in this country. But I do wish you did not have to go so far away.

I saved the best news for last. When I told Father you were in London I asked him if he thought it was possible for me to go visit you. I thought he would say, "No, your mother and I would never let you go so far away by yourself." But instead he said he would give it some thought.

After I came upstairs, while I have been sitting at the table writing to you, Father knocked on the door. He came in my room and said, "I was thinking about your making a visit to London. I am not saying positively that you can go, but I will look into it and make inquiries. We might try to make arrangements with some of our

British friends. Of course I'll have to talk to your mother about this." Then he laughed and said if I went I better not get seasick. I could hardly believe my ears!

I hope this letter finds you well. The next time you hear from me, Father might be persuaded to let me come visit you!

Your friend,

Abby

As Louisa read about Abby visiting her father's grave, her hands started to tremble. But when she got to the end of the letter, she let out a cry (to no one in particular), "Abby's coming to London!" Abby's father had all but promised her he would make it possible. The news was almost too good to be true.

When Abby came to London, there would be so many people to see and places to go. Louisa had so much to tell Abby. It would be just like old times. Then Louisa pictured the visit ending. Abby would return to Washington, bringing flowers to the grave and a message for Louisa's mother. "I saw your daughter. Things are going well. She's free now." *And yet*, Louisa thought, *not so free that I can go home again.*

Still, the city of London lay before her. Within a few months Louisa would help Bernice and Samuel open their shop. In the meantime she liked working for Lady Baxter. After all the housekeeper always looked out for her and often saved her a slice of plum cake. Louisa had to admit it tasted every bit as good as Mrs. Bailey's cinnamon coach wheels.

Louisa folded the letter and put it back in her pocket. Roy would be there soon. She couldn't wait to show him her letter.

Postscript

The story of *Freedom Calls* takes place at a time when Washington was a small city, and a new one, built along the swampy banks of the Potomac and Anacostia Rivers. Tension over slavery ran high, often at fever pitch, whether in the halls of Congress, in shops or taverns, in church pulpits or marketplaces, in the mansions of the rich, or the homes of the poor. Indeed many African Americans had already taken back their freedom and the free blacks far outnumbered the slaves. (The 1840 census counted 30,657 whites, 8,361 free blacks, and 4,694 slaves.) Many slaves fled north, finding freedom once they crossed the border into Pennsylvania or New Jersey.

Much of what happened in this book is fact and some is fiction. On the night of April 15, 1848, seventy-six slaves (including thirteen children), belonging to forty-one prominent families, did secretly board the *Pearl* at a Washington harbor. (One of the fugitives, Ellen, was owned by the former First Lady Dolley Madison.) Daniel Drayton, Captain Sayres, and the hired cook Chester

English sailed the boat down the Potomac River, 130 miles into the Chesapeake Bay, docking at Cornfield Harbor. The *Pearl* was captured in the early hours of the morning on the seventeenth. The posse, led by young Francis Dodge of Georgetown, brought the slaves back to Washington. Few owners took their slaves back; most sold them to the slave dealers in Baltimore, Annapolis, Alexandria, and Richmond. Slaves bought by Bruin and Hill were sent to New Orleans to be auctioned.

Paul Edmondson, the father of Emily and Mary who appear in *Freedom Calls*, was successful in raising the money needed to buy his daughters' freedom. The girls later enrolled at Oberlin College, one of the first integrated academic institutions in the country. Mary, her health weakened by imprisonment in the slave pen, died that year. Emily returned to Washington to teach at a school opened by Myrtilla Miner, the first in the city for African Americans.

Daniel Drayton and Captain Sayres remained in jail while both Horace Mann and Charles Sumner (an abolitionist elected to the Senate in 1851) fought for them to receive a presidential pardon. In real life there was a Mr. Wood who visited Daniel Drayton in jail and taught him to read and write. He was not a young reporter for the *National Era*, but a clerk in the telegraph office.

In 1852, President Millard Fillmore issued a pardon, freeing the two captains after four years, four months,

and seven days in prison. Eager to escape the possibility
of a retrial in Virginia (where two of the fugitive slaves
had lived), they fled Washington as quickly as possible.
Lewis Clephane, business manager of the *National Era,*
arranged for a driver to take them to Baltimore where
they could catch the train to Philadelphia.

Three years later, Daniel Drayton published his life
story, the *Personal Memoir of Daniel Drayton.* In it he
concludes that he acted not for personal gain, but as a
"protest against the infamous and atrocious doctrine that
there can be any such thing as property in man... It was
impossible that I should ever be able to make myself heard
in Congress, or by the nation at large, except in the way of
action."

While in Congress, Horace Mann devoted himself to
anti-slavery issues. He also actively promoted better
education and supported improved care for the mentally
ill. In 1852, Mr. Mann left politics and helped found
Antioch College in Ohio, a non-sectarian institution open
to both men and women, and to all races.

Later in life, Daniel Drayton's prosecutor Philip
Barton Key (son of Francis Scott Key, the author of "The
Star-Spangled Banner") would again figure prominently
in the pages of the Washington newspapers. In 1858, Mr.
Key fell in love with the wife of a New York congressman.
When the congressman learned of his wife's infidelity, he
shot Mr. Key three times in the back, killing his rival.

Newspaper accounts of the period, Daniel Drayton's memoir, Horace Mann's letters, and *Fugitives of the Pearl*, a book written in 1930 by John H. Paynter, a descendant of two of the slaves on the *Pearl*, have all chronicled the escape of the slaves aboard the *Pearl*. For *Freedom Calls* portions of the testimony and opening statements during the trial were adapted from court records.

Gamaliel and Margaret Bailey met in Cincinnati, Ohio, where Dr. Bailey became publisher of the *Philanthropist*, the first abolitionist newspaper in the Midwest. The Baileys later moved to Washington to continue their anti-slavery work. They had twelve children, six of whom survived. Margaret edited a juvenile anti-slavery magazine called *Youth's Monthly Visitor* (with a circulation of three thousand). Gamaliel published the first issue of the *National Era* on January 7, 1847. This weekly abolitionist newspaper included the work of John Greenleaf Whittier and Sara Jane Clarke (the Baileys' governess who wrote under the pen name of Grace Greenwood). As portrayed in *Freedom Calls* Dr. Bailey was accused of masterminding the plot of the slaves' escape aboard the *Pearl* and an anti-abolitionist mob came to his house to threaten him.

In 1851, Dr. Bailey paid Harriet Beecher Stowe one hundred dollars to write a short story for the paper. She submitted the first installment of *Uncle Tom's Cabin*; this appeared in print on June 5, 1851. The response was so great that Dr. Bailey sent another one hundred dollars with a request for a second installment. She kept writing in installments; the last was published in the *National Era* on May 1, 1852.

Unfortunately Gamaliel Bailey did not live to witness the end of slavery. Gamaliel, who suffered a digestive disorder called dyspepsia, took an ocean voyage to improve his health. He died at sea on June 5, 1859, while aboard the *Arago*.

Although the Baileys never had a daughter named Abigail, and very little is known about the children they did have, I tried to imagine how the world would have appeared to a fourteen-year-old daughter of the *National Era* publisher. What might her experiences have been?

There was no girl named Louisa in the records of the slaves aboard the *Pearl*. She also is a product of my imagination. The story of what happened to her is—I hope—as near to truth as any history that has been written.

Of the approximately one hundred thousand slaves who escaped from slavery in the United States, a great many found refuge in northern states. Others reached Canada, while a smaller, yet significant number fled to Great Britain. The world they discovered was not unlike the one Louisa found. Often former slaves gave lectures throughout the British Isles to further the abolitionist cause. Such African American speakers included the great orator Frederick Douglass; the author William Wells Brown; Samuel Ringgold Ward, a Congregationalist minister and agent for the New York Anti-Slavery Society; Josiah Henson, the minister who built housing for a fugitive community in Dawn, Ontario; and William and Ellen Craft, who escaped slavery in Georgia. This husband and wife team traveled in disguise, Ellen dressed as a master, and her husband as the servant. The autobiographies of these fugitives helped me in many ways to imagine Louisa's life in England.

Like many fugitives who came to Britain and stayed, Louisa paid a dear price for liberty. She left behind family, friends, and home. But she knew she made the right choice.

Author's Note

While working on *Freedom Calls: Journey of a Slave Girl*, I read the handwritten court records of Captain Drayton's trial at the National Archives and located the unmarked graves of Gamaliel and Margaret Bailey's family at the Oak Hill Cemetery in Georgetown. I walked along the banks of the Potomac River and on the very streets where the Baileys, the 76 slaves, and their captors once lived, and I traveled to Cornfield Harbor, a secluded cove near Point Lookout on the Chesapeake Bay, where the *Pearl* was captured. All these experiences helped me in imagining the lives of Abby and Louisa.

I conducted my research at the Historical Society of Washington, D.C., the Library of Congress, the Martin Luther King Memorial Library, the Moorland Spingarn Research Center at Howard University, and the Cleveland Park and Georgetown public libraries. I would like to thank the many people there for giving me access to slave narratives, memoirs, and newspaper accounts of the period as well as for providing me with a welcome place to work.

180

I am also most grateful to Harold Collier at White Mane, and to Alice Powers, Antonio Alcala, Pat Taylor, and Hilary Cairns. Special thanks to my husband, Jon, and to our three daughters Kate, Eve, and Ida for giving me good advice and, most of all, for always believing in this project.